Psyche *of* Mirrors

Psyche of Mirrors

A PROMENADE OF PORTRAITS

CAROLYN MARY KLEEFELD

Myths are waiting for our imaginations to breathe life into them.
—Albert Camus

The Seventh Quarry &
Cross-Cultural Communications
Wales / New York
2012

Several of the poems in this collection have been published in previous books by the author. Poems have also appeared in *The Seventh Quarry Swansea Poetry Magazine* (Wales), *Voices Israel* and *Cyclamens and Swords* (Israel), *Convorbiri Literare, Poesis, Poezia, Citadela, Contemporanul, Ideea Europeana,* and *Acolada* (Romania, tr. Dr. Olimpia Iacob), *Korean Expatriate Literature* and *The Big Sur Round-Up* (USA).

Inquiries about *Psyche of Mirrors* should be addressed to

Editor-Publisher: **Peter Thabit Jones**
The Seventh Quarry Press
Dan-y-bryn, 74 Cwm Level Road
Brynhyfryd, Swansea SA5 9DY Wales
info@peterthabitjones.com
www.peterthabitjones.com

Editor-Publisher: **Stanley H. Barkan**
Cross-Cultural Communications
239 Wynsum Avenue
Merrick, New York 11566-4725 USA
(516) 868-5635
(516) 379-1901 fax
cccpoetry@aol.com
www.cross-culturalcommunications.com

Inquiries about the author's artwork, fine art cards, and other books should be addressed to

Atoms Mirror Atoms, Inc.
PO Box 221693
Carmel, California 93922 USA
(800) 403-3635
(831) 667-2433
info@carolynmarykleefeld.com
www.carolynmarykleefeld.com

Friend Carolyn Mary Kleefeld on Facebook

Library of Congress Control Number: 2011941741
ISBN 978-0-89304-361-2

Book and cover design by Li Yao
Art photography and photograph of the author by Dennis Wyszynski
For cover art, see Paintings, page 221

First Printing 2012
Printed in Canada

Contents

Chapter 1 · Orphic Lovers

Chapter 2 · The Beast Within

Chapter 3 · Homage to Silence

CHAPTER 4 · PARADOXICAL POSES

CHAPTER 5 · GRIST FOR THE SPIRITUAL MILL

CHAPTER 6 · QUINTESSENTIAL CREATORS

CHAPTER 7 · VISAGES OF DEATH

CHAPTER 8 · EPIPHANIES

Painting at David's

ACKNOWLEDGMENTS

My endless love, gratitude, and blessings to all I acknowledge here, who have so generously brought their inspiration, vision, talents, devotion, and confidence toward the achievement of this book, which has been twenty-five years in creation.

To the beloved and quintessential godmothers of *Psyche of Mirrors: A Promenade of Portraits,* I am ever grateful:

Patricia Holt for her sacrosanct and valiant being, editorial brilliance, mystical connection to my work, and undaunted devotion that made this publication possible.

Kirtana, Wild Dove, for her clarity of being, editorial and organizational genius, supreme patience, and sacred devotion to my life's work.

With ever-abiding appreciation to my chosen brother and publisher, Stanley H. Barkan, for his invaluable editorial acuity and confidence in my work.

To John Dotson, most treasured catalyst, for his editorial perspectives and unwavering support in a myriad of essential ways.

To Peter Thabit Jones, my dearest poet-brother, for his priest-like dedication and over the moon support of my life's work. To Vince Clemente, my spiritual father, for his profound influence in my life. And to Deanna McKinstry Edwards, radiant songbird, for her insightful preface.

To David Wayne Dunn, for the essential difference he has made in my life and for his extra special inspiration.

In memory of my beloved friend and muse Laura Archera Huxley, whose contribution to my life and work is ever cherished and celebrated.

To Piero Ferrucci, for his most valued friendship and meaningful response to this work.

To John Larson, the guardian of Pankosmion and patient Noah of the Ark, for his extraordinary devotion and support.

To Laura Zabrowski for her awesome assistance and dedication.

To Li Yao for her exceptional diligence and most creative cover and book design.

To Ronna Emmons, Natalie Van Allen, Martin Shears, Dennis Wyszynski, and Professor Doctor Bernfried Nugel for their continuing special support.

To David Campagna, my deepest gratitude for our sacred kinship and cherished inspiration.

For Leonard Cohen, who connects his primal well of being with his tower of sublime song.

To Travis Kleefeld, Carla Kleefeld and Celeste Worl, Claudia and Chiara Kleefeld, Valerie Corral, Dr. Roberta Spurr, Dr. Roy Auerbach, Linda Jacobson, David Jay Brown, Robert Edwards, Bebe Barkan, Lorena Del Campo, John Schneider, Peggy and George DiCaprio, Dr. Paul Fleiss, Nick Frangakis, Dr. Ralph Potkin and Eugenia Galvas, Butch Shuman, Chungliang Al Huang, Karen Pfeiffer and Kyla, Evan Landy, Jai Italiander and Jamie Roth, Frank Zabrowski, Terry Prince and Rachel Moody, Glen Cheda, Edna Isman, Barbara and David Simonich, Melissa Goese-Goble, Linda Parker, Marla Bell, and Gail Bengard for their much valued support.

And to my mentors and comrades who inspire beyond death, Dr. Carl Faber, Edmund Kara, Barry Taper, Freda Taper, Dr. Timothy Leary, Dr. Oscar Janiger, Terence McKenna, Nina Graboi, Dr. John Lilly, William Melamed, and the unnamed others.

For my parents, "Pops" Mark Taper and Amelia, for creating me and making so much possible, and for the generations of ancestors who pulse on through me. I am ever humbled and grateful.

PREFACE

I feel the title *Psyche of Mirrors* and subtitle *A Promenade of Portraits* create a structure. They also thread the different forms—prose-pieces, mini-short stories, journal-type entries, poems, and paintings.

This is a remarkable and original manuscript, indeed, the creative result of "the offbeat alleys of peculiar and revealing realms." For example, "Black Panther on a Leash" is as good as any of the prose-pieces in Charles Baudelaire's ground-breaking *Paris Spleen*.

I love the Jonathan Swift-like qualities of some of the prose, reality wrapped up in fantasy, and I love its Lewis Carroll mischievousness. I also love the Lawrencian prose-pieces, which are honest, naked, questioning, and—for me at least—come from a realization that all life is touched by an eternal grief, indeed "engraving her soul with sorrow."

It is an outstanding journey of a book, a journey that is humorous, sad, profound, searching, calm, and restless. It is also a journal of a true visionary, and the work of an imagination overflowing, an imagination at times overpowered by the inner and outer worlds.

It has so many striking pieces, and so many freshly-baked lines that any writer would give their left arm to have under his or her name. "And the harvest moon / threatens to burst with / all her silvery secrets, / letting them fall to earth / like love letters written / to our beseeching souls." Wow! They are lines that stick like burrs in the mind. This is a work that is a treasure-chest of many things, yet all stamped with Carolyn's distinctive and arresting voice.

Her soul, whether aching or bubbling with joy, sings through the array of works. She sees into the heart of things, be it the world called reality or the other, more eternal world. Most writers look into the mirror of being to be self-pleased, to be confirmed as one who is just like the others, to be reassured like a child that one is not alone. Like the seer that she is, Carolyn looks into the mirrors of truths, whether they soothe or sting her human fragility. That unflinching searching makes all the great writers worth reading so brave, and Carolyn is so brave.

Like Lawrence, Van Gogh, and Blake, her imagination is ablaze with so many ideas and insights. This manuscript allows us to glimpse some of the people and (nature's) furniture of an incredible mind. She is "an anarchist behind the scenes," rather than "a redundant 'reproducer' of familiar realities."

She always controls her material with a craft-aware care, be it the factual "An Artist's Impressions of Big Sur" or the mystical "The Fallen Star."

I love the poems, which would make a very strong collection on their own; and I love the paintings, the way they complement and expand the writings. There is so much to praise in this manuscript;

to pick out some is really unfair to the others. However, I must mention the beautiful, controlled "A Realm Birthed in Silence." And "Halloween Musings on the Nature of Creativity" is such a wonderful and very original evocation of the ambiguity and the irony for the creator in creating something.

I thank the gods for this "world-stranger." Literature needs those prepared to stand outside the organized movie of life, to see its many aspects of absurdity against everlasting time and a universe yawning away for aeons.

Peter Thabit Jones
Swansea, Wales
2011

Peter Thabit Jones is a poet, publisher, and author of *The Lizard Catchers, The Boy and the Lion's Head,* and *Poems from a Cabin on Big Sur,* among others.

INTRODUCTION

Psyche of Mirrors is a sonorous volume, a breviary of sorts, of tightly woven *poems* as in "I Found My Soul," *prose poems* like "Gossamer Memories," *parables* as in "This Part of Her Arm," *conversations with the self,* and *hymnals* as in "O Night, My Ebony Master."

The volume sings with a voice often reaching Whitman's *Orchards of the Spheres,* and evoking the Zen tradition of Wabi—what my old friend, poet, and translator, Lucien Stryk defines in his masterwork *Zen Poems of China and Japan* as "The feeling of something hitherto ignored suddenly being seen for the precious thing it is and always has been, though hidden from us by illusion."

This volume is such a work of "wakening," of immersing a startled reader in this very *Holy Fount* that is the natural world we *saunter* through, and Carolyn Kleefeld, always with an eye to the word's thumbprint through time, *saunters,* "along a sacred place," while staring into the very countenance of life's pulsating enigma.

Psyche of Mirrors begins with an Albert Camus quote: "Myths are waiting for our imaginations to breathe life into them." And such imaginations, soul-deep life breath, impregnate these myths, these very dark recesses of life's perplexing, however hallowed nature. How I appreciate, value, the volume's "painter's finder" lens through which to study, experience such a universe, its very flight of passage through time. The line from Camus seems to ask the reader to come to terms with what he insisted is life's very absurdity, and the human attempt—often a struggle—at clarity and synthesis and celebration, qualities one blissfully experiences in this remarkable volume, its form, prosody, and vision.

What is most salient of this breviary is, as I have discovered, its variety of forms. To begin with the poetry, I have chosen to focus on the volume's final work, "I Found My Soul." And I ask, how many of us would dare explore such a revelation. Carolyn Kleefeld is, then, writer as courage-teacher, as was Emily Dickinson, and of course, I have in mind a poem like her "Presentiment" that concludes, "Notice to the startled grass that darkness is about to pass." And you here too! "I Found My Soul" finds the speaker whispering, as if we eavesdrop:

> In the grace of
> a dying garden,
> I found my soul.

Of course the resonant word is grace, found even in a "dying garden," and I recall Pascal's "The motions of grace, the hardness of the heart. . . ." But in Carolyn Kleefeld, never this hardness of the heart, simply the courage and faith to be, as she finds herself in the poem's penultimate stanza, indeed in this, *Holy Fount,* there in Nature's amniotic fluids. We read along with her:

> I swim in the old pool
> with new water and
> the light of the future
> beams through the boughs
> of ancient oak.

This is a literal pool, but the "new water" is sacrosanct liquid to birth a soul, to braid one with the timelessness of "boughs / of ancient oak." The poem ends, as does the volume, in a tercet, each line concluding with a resonating sibilant:

> Old and new fuse
> in my bloodstreams—
> in the primal waters.

As we read, the speaker now is fused with "bloodstreams," and like the Zen master Yuishun, she is "Awakened at last, / . . . the moon / Above the pines, the river surging high."

As an example of a prose poem, "Gossamer Memories," in its brevity and life-piercing imagery and vision, reveals a profound, enduring memory of the human need to "reach for the stars." We hear initially how "Last night we were breathed by the stars, the ancient lords of mystery, the ebony glittering dome." And how the speaker, with a trusted companion, "imbibed the wine of lunar enchantment, the shadows, the flowering seas." And we learn how such absorption of the truly human in the truly transcendental makes us "more than we had been."

And all this is now part of the sacred vessel of memory, and caressed in these very "invisible cloaks of blessing, we watch as the fog drifts in, obscuring the heavens, enshrouding the trees with veils of lavender mist." This "lavender mist" of such a star-drifting universe, is, again, answer to the volume's lens of voice of Albert Camus: "Myths are waiting for our imaginations to breathe life into them."

And the parable "This Part of Her Arm" is written, I'm certain, with an eye to the word's "fossil truth," back to the Middle English *parabile,* "allegory for teaching spiritual truth." "This Part of Her Arm" is just a six-line narrative, yet allegorical in its nature, worth reading in its entirety:

> "This part of my arm," she exclaimed, "is innocent, untouched. It
> has never been part of the world. It thrives in childhood's bramble
> and bees, in the fawn, the visiting bird and the light-heartedness of
> youth. Yes, this part of my arm," she repeated, "is innocent."

Then he kissed her little hand and sprinkled water on her dear, little arm. And she became innocent again.

This terse, understated narrative conveys a "spiritual truth," the sanctity of the human body, as it conveys all heaven and earth in its cage of impermanent form. And to think, here for us in a single woman's arm, witness to "childhood's bramble and bees . . . light-heartedness of youth." And there are many such other parables awaiting a reader about to be anointed.

And finally, the volume's hymnals, as in "O Night, My Ebony Master," evoking such a beckoning prayer with each line, a genuflecting, verbal, antiphonal cadence that captures the very sonic nature of hymnals. We first hear

O night, whose darkness I inhabit, let the seeds that thrive in
your womb of sea inseminate me, resurrecting me as the bud
before spring.

It is to become, then, this prayer of resurrection, and so like Carolyn Kleefeld, she reaches for a metaphor that will braid her to the very piety of the natural world, to be born as this very "bud before spring."

And always in the hymnal, this chorus of antiphonal cadences resounds; just listen to each line's awakening voice:

O darkness that feeds my blindness with vision . . .
Come to me, wingéd ebony lord, master of my flesh's glory . . .
I await you, dearest master of my dry heart's love . . .
How long shall I wait, O seeds of night . . .

And the hymnal concludes in hushed silence, ". . . bring your tawny arms to me while on Earth we still be." One may only conclude with the word, Amen.

And finally, the compelling paintings. Carolyn Kleefeld is both an accomplished writer and artist, indeed a unique talent, one I'm sure to endure. I am no art critic, yet each painting only enhances the written texts, reaches out to its reader, whispering, "Yet there is more," and this "more" is, for me at least, a return to the Zen tradition, this time to that of the Chinese and Japanese master painters. I read through this volume, pause, entering the life of each painting, recall works of Zen masters, like Shinso, his *Landscape;* Sesshu, his *Ink-Splash Landscape* and *Winter Landscape;* Ryozen, his *White*

Heron; and finally, Niten, whose *Crow on the Pine Branch* most evokes the images that only deepen one's immersion in this modern masterpiece, *Psyche of Mirrors: A Promenade of Portraits.*

Vince Clemente
New York, New York
2011

Vince Clemente is Professor Emeritus of English, State University of New York, poet, biographer, and author of *John Ciardi: Measure of the Man* and *The Heartbreak at the Heart of Things,* among others.

FOREWORD

In *Psyche of Mirrors,* Carolyn Mary Kleefeld writes with an enormous generosity of spirit, creating a unique and enchanting promenade for the many voices of the soul. As I read these portraits, I met a great deal of myself and was considerably roused and affected.

I was also struck by how musical this promenade of portraits is. Carolyn often writes with an acoustic sense of things. Many cosmologies begin with the universe coming into being through sound. For example, Rudolf Steiner and Don Campbell see the soul as tone, which means the psyche is a musical instrument, as is the body. I love these words of George Leonard, "Before we make music, music makes us." Poets like Carolyn, who feel the numinous in nature, bring that music to life in their poetry.

In this personal yet universal promenade, Carolyn never removes herself or her characters from the tensions that polarities impart to life. This, in fact, is one of her themes, that everything we encounter in our interior and exterior world mirrors back to our souls this dance of polarities. Carolyn imaginatively interprets these seemingly opposing voices through each of her characters. In turn, she becomes the female Schnoozler, Dahlia, Izabella, Lisa-Fleur, Extra-Vera. She is the troubled one and the rescuer. She's all the lovers, one moment smoothed out by love, the next shaken and searching for what went wrong. In her fantasies, Carolyn allows all the seeming paradoxes of life to belong to each other, to wrestle and thrive in each other's company.

She intimates that not to acknowledge, even honor, these polar energies can be construed as an ecological misstep for the soul desiring wholeness. If one is open enough to hold life's seeming, teeming, and unsettling paradoxes, sometimes one can churn into our many selves a honey of well-being that sustains and transforms the tempests of our fiery universe at play within and without.

And if one thinks of Psyche and Eros, the myth which James Hillman holds to be *the* myth of our time, then any promenade of Psyche will be saturated with Eros. Carolyn walks into this realm and the endless images residing here with an unflinchingly intrepid and questing mind/heart. She sows into each of her portraits all the emotional intentions, tenderness, tensions, and courage it took dear Psyche to sort all those seeds, crying to the weeds by the river, almost throwing herself in, but finally and ultimately meeting love's dark beauties and dazzling grace to fly like an eagle.

Psyche of Mirrors is a magical multitude of nurturing voices and playful hands for your own soul's promenade, a romp kindled through with Eros and his tumults. Hers is the dialogue we all engage in, one way or another, the one between the world as it presents itself visibly and the world as it whispers and roars invisibly within our souls, upsetting best laid plans, troubling us, but also lifting us in rapture.

Deanna McKinstry-Edwards, PhD
Carmel, California
2010

Deanna McKinstry-Edwards is an actress, singer, and author of *Psyche, Eros, and Me*.

CHAPTER 1

ORPHIC LOVERS

Eros and Aphrodite

LOVER BORNE OF SILENCE

I sink deeper into
a sea of silence
where I find you
wading through the currents,
your arms reaching out for me
as if you knew I'd be there
looking for you.

As we drink in the twilight calm,
our orange hearts guide us
through sap green cypress
guarding our path,
cloaking us in the gossamer
of falling darkness,
where we find each other anew
in the fleeting moment.

Although our dream
has now vanished
into the mist,
your essence lingers
in the fathomless stillness,
my eternal beloved,
my sacred companion.

2011

LOVERS WALK BY THE SEA

The full moon, like a beacon of wisdom, beams through the torpid gray, imbibing earthly life into its orb, its cool, iridescent wine.

Remote and indifferent, this ancient, sovereign goddess drinks in the passions and woes of the beseeching souls below, staring blindly at all, even at those not gazing. As a luminous vessel, she appears full, yet her soul is forever empty with an insatiable drought, not unlike the souls of the striving civilization below, whose miseries are cast off in superfluous synthetics.

While the fluorescent lights of those without vision burn on beneath her in a plastic world, the moon, with her streaming tresses cast, coolly mocks the artificial glare. She muses that courageous explorers who rely on their *inner* sun can germinate the seeds of pollen's light, traveling the lunar paths of imagination, discovering unfamiliar realms, as did the ancient, distance-traveling Hindus.

And wandering lovers stroll on by the sea, past a harbor of yachts; their shimmering reflections dance mutely amidst the ebony shadows. Trees bow gracefully in their storm-soaked, wintry garments. The young woman gazes into the lunar radiance, feeling distant, yet mysteriously more intimate with her lover, rhapsodically drawn to the stars of eternity glittering in his eyes.

The trees in their dormant nakedness make promises to her soul of the approaching spring. The roar of the primordial ocean merges with the barks of sea lions.

The lovers continue to wander through the raw bite of a January night with its distant blinking lights. And the moon soars on, as do the lovers, unknowingly.

2001

HEAVEN'S ENVY

for John Hall Wheelock

The heavens are envious
of our love.
After all, they are so removed.

The gardens of Earth
are quite drunk
with their own lushness.

Even the seas have
lost their patience
with forever being water.

At dawn, the stars
are finally released
from their guardian,
while you and I
stroll down our paths
in wonder and relief
that for these moments
the gods rejoice in us.

Reverent is the beetle
that crosses our road—
in awe of the Riddle
that put him here.

Locked in their petals,
daisies smile when the moon
softens their prisons.

And the fish
of all our remorse
surpass themselves,
leaping out of
the dancing waves,
sure in those seconds
to celebrate.

2011

THE SCHNOOZLER PETS

The Schnoozlers are known to be unique, a love-matched pair, reclusive, and a great source of mystery to those who meet them. Being dramatic of personality, they are disinterested and bored by consensus reality. They know better; they are the Sublime Pets. Discriminating in their interests and how they spend their time, they make the sensual and erotic their priority.

The Schnoozlers believe there is no better way to start the day than to wake up and melt into each other's ecstatic bliss. From there, the clearest, highest visions will lens the day. With their long, furry muzzles and beaks, the Schnoozlers love to snuggle around and in every corner of their faces, ears, and necks.

They enjoy having intimate frolicking parties for each other where they play spacy hi-tech music and lose their conceptual minds to the unlimited, where creativity thrives. Both are inventing all the time, metamorphosing through their unbridled imaginations.

The female, Ms. Schnoozler-Pet, exclaims that most people are so mired in social reality retro-memes,[1] the conditioning from emotional germs, that they have no new ideas, just imitations of old ones. Ms. Schnoozler-Pet prefers experimenting from the non-conceptual wilderness realm. To her, memes pollute the sacrosanct.

It is said that the female Schnoozler is far more susceptible to contagious social concepts than the male. Before she met her male Schnoozler, she had lived amidst the movie business in Hollywood and had been seduced countless times by the advertised realities. As a result, her visions had temporarily dissipated. For a while she had found these realities to be engaging, but then had become disenchanted and recognized it was only her imagination that had made them seem interesting. At this point, they were only worthwhile for dissecting and understanding from a psychological or philosophical stance.

Both Ms. Schnoozler and her lover pet Schnoozler are discerning in using their energy not only sensually but also with the additional priority of creating from their highest ideals. The male Schnoozler specializes in computer technology designed to alleviate the drain of mundane and repetitious tasks and thus free up energy for higher priorities. And the female Schnoozler, through her artwork, creates symbolic expressions of a transcendent realm—one of myth through which all innocence and wonder is birthed and thrives.

The Schnoozlers are very fortunate to live on a mountain cliff high above the sea with their own pristine, sandy cove below. They are surrounded by blossoming, sun-rich fruits, vines of roses, jasmine, and honeysuckle. When the tropical breezes blow, the Schnoozlers inhale intoxicating, aphrodisiacal gardens, and exhale freshly born images and forms.

A distinguishing feature of the female Schnoozler is her unusually fine, silky, electric fur of medium length, which sticks out and seems to purr softly. Her feet and hands have angora mauve fur, and her feathered mane is a bright magenta. She has long, horse-like ears with white downy fur inside. She walks on shapely legs and has hummingbird wings of various purple shades that change designs like a chameleon. A rare mixture of horse and bird—from the waist down, she is horsepower; from the waist up, hummingbird.

Her lover pet Schnoozler is mostly of the bird species. But he is also dragon and occasionally has a touch of some furry, cozy creature that hasn't yet been identified. His wide wings are woven of purple and lilac feathers, which are sensitive to his physical environment and the best flight strategies. He keeps his feathers clean and fresh, lucid for flight.

"There are many eyes in his feathers," his lover Schnoozler murmurs. "Perhaps he is a relative of the peacock, although he doesn't appear at all conceited."

It is said that the female Schnoozler lives her visions somatically, sensing life through the countless silken antennae of her fur. The great movie screen of life continually blueprints her infinite cellular canvases. After absorbing these impressions, she then can express her artistic interpretations from the molecular level to canvas or paper.

The Schnoozlers chose a colossal redwood tree for their home, with a sequence of rustic chambers connected by 102 doors, and with towering portals through which they can fly. The female Schnoozler believes that these openings are manifestations of the myriad, vibrant perceptions and expanded dimensions she and her lover Schnoozler experience living together. This nest-tower has many fragranced vines intertwining their chamber's labyrinths. Trees burgeon through the many open atriums. And crystalline mosaic windows reveal extensive panoramas.

Their chambers are molecular and organic, vibrantly pulsing—moving, breathing, and opening with every new wave of perception. Deeply connected in the infinite Cosmic Loom, their pollinated selves spin threads of gold, unfurling like filigree from their ever-expanding vision.

1985

A SLAVE TO THIS CALLING
for David

I'm seeing things and feeling things in whole new ways. Your presence enters my marrow, and I am fed by you on an invisible level. The timeless awaits my mind's liberation as I brim with the seeds you plant both in act and thought, until you become a part of me, blossoming and exploding like an unfamiliar flower, adding petals and stem—a mutant borne of passion.

A slave to this calling, this urgent love, I am on my knees before the mystery, all of me in this dance, answering to love.

2012

OUR WOVEN TERRACE TO THE STARS

Our woven terrace
led to the stars.
Below, a lush forest of fragrant
fig and plum trees blossomed,
their seeds exploding in the heat.

When you held me
tightly in your arms,
the fire of our fulfillment
melted any separation,
and every enchanted moment
led to new wonders.

Now that you have departed,
I feast on the memories
of our intimate adventure.

Our terrace led to the stars.
And so did you.
I took your lead,
and some secret realm
was discovered.

We became ever closer
while the forests burgeoned
and the heavens bloomed
from our fertile seed within.

2011

Erotic Rendezvous

A DIONYSIAN NIGHT

Fueled by the sheer joy of creating, he and his lover used themselves as media for their art, love, and passion. He was an avant-garde artist of numerous expressions who resided in a commune-like complex where his neighbors slept and lived a traditional lifestyle. It was a mystery, the myriad facets of their lives, the ebb and flow of their connection. Here they were, painting, dancing, and singing— primal spirits, gypsies ancient and contemporary, living and creating beyond the conditioned.

For these two artists, ignited by the erotic blaze of passion, this Dionysian night was like no other. Their sublime moments outside of time exploded into existence, to be assimilated and re-alchemized later, as mulch for further creative experiments.

He made videos of her creative fugue, the vatic dance of her brushes upon the canvas. In her black lingerie and low décolletage, she improvised, applying paint wildly with wire brushes that punctuated the short video with sharp, scratchy sounds.

It was a halcyon night, birthed from the subterranean, where the amber lights of their souls merged with the red and white flames of passion in a dance from the edge of the creative cliffs. Mysteriously, without knowing it, each had created the portrait-essence of the other, each from an echoing mirror within.

2009

WHERE SECRETS GROW
for David

I discover you at last
in that wondrous place
where secrets grow.

You've come.
And the silver moons
with their red lips
sing from your lyrical soul.

At last, the gods are kind,
letting us luxuriate—
you inside me,
I, a reflecting star,
silvery, sensuous, erotic.

You emerge from
where secrets grow.
And life begins and ends with you
as you throb through
my rivers of longing,
filling me with seeds
of fertile passion,
colors of harvest—
the music that you are.

2010

DAHLIA AND DOMINICK

Across the English countryside, the rain pounded relentlessly with a heavy dullness, numb with the world's travails, as if it could never heal the Earth from the abuse of its human inhabitants.

Yet sequestered in a forest green lived a white, long-limbed creature named Dahlia, the guardian of flowers, who seemed oblivious to the rain. She lived there with a brown monkey called Safari and a female Afghan puppy named Cleo. These two matched her high-strung nature and flowing, sand-colored tresses. But her favorite pet, even more exotic than the others, was a puma-like musician named Dominick Ferraro, who, after living for many years as a Bohemian in Prague, had settled nearby.

A sensitive and reclusive creature, Dahlia nevertheless enjoyed intricate and meaningful relationships with people. Her preference was to withdraw from a busy social existence in order to have as much time as possible to paint, draw, and write. But her creativity was constantly invaded. Dominick brought her the only music that inspired, music of the senses, of passion.

Dominick was tall, muscular of limb, with the powerful thighs of a runner. There was something unusual about him. His ancestors were Persian and deeply religious. An ancient aura emanated from his golden-brown skin, and his dark-brown, penetrating eyes revealed a deep connection to the Earth. He wore a seductive and exotic blend of oils behind his ears. When they were especially intimate, his altars of desire were illumined as if with endless rows of glowing candles lit within his chest.

Dahlia was comfortable with both his primitive simplicity and his deep, intuitive, cosmologic philosophy. Then again, when he acted from his more primal nature, he could be altogether abrasive and invasive. Dominick epitomized incredible contradictions. And together Dahlia and Dominick embodied and multiplied their individual paradoxes.

As they strolled along a lonely forest road, Dominick exclaimed to Dahlia, "Physical love is *everything*—nothing else really matters." They paused under the towering trees and gazed into the twilight of each other's souls.

"Why not live from that priority," she said, "and do everything we can to deepen that intimacy." They agreed to run their lives around the making of love in all its myriad forms. And from their flame of passion, they could inspire their souls, their artwork, and perhaps, the world.

2002

ANOTHER REALM ENTERS

My river flows into the sea again
where golden tortoises behold me
with ancient eyes.

Soon, a deep sea-diver appears,
bringing treasures untold.

I disrobe before his sea-green self
and melt into his wavering fronds.

Out of his unclenched fists,
secrets drift into the open sea.

I glide from his seductive arms
and swim amongst his gifts,
imbibing them hungrily.

I sense them within myself,
as if another realm had entered,
creating gems in me never known before.

But suddenly the sea evaporates,
and the deep-sea diver vanishes.

Then I hear mysterious music
emanating from the navel of
a brown-skinned man
who flies through the air on a flute.

Climbing onto his resonant notes,
I clasp him in my blood.
And yet another realm enters.

2008

THEY WERE POETS TOGETHER

Raging like a bull, he banged on every door he could find, ready to break them all down to get to her. Finally, he came blasting in.

She had needed a night of darkness to bathe in, a respite from the chaos that had beset her world. Her once quiet home, her sanctuary, now felt threatened.

He was continually restless, in a state of disquiet and suffering, but he hadn't always been that way. Oh, how they had loved, and oh, how they had soared.

What had changed? They had once transcended mortal love and breathed of the meadows of eternity. They had been poets and muses together, living in a realm only they could spin and inhabit, writing wondrous poems inspired by each other. What had happened?

What was all the tumult and bickering about? Was it because they were chameleons and it was time for change, for more expansive relationships? How much of the agitation came from the world at large, as archetypal dynamics expressed through them?

She was weary of so-called love. But what else was there to live for, to breathe from?

How could love play such tricks on them, squeezing the last grape in their winepress, leaving them bloodless and pathetic?

He had been a Pan, her unfallen god of nature, her passionate soul-comrade. And now, the sweet dream had become bitter.

She knew that life was filled with contradiction. Was she a part of him reflected? Why was she surprised and bewildered?

Even in the beginning, in the mad heat of their full moon's dawn, he was always leaving (but never for long). And slowly, she had adapted to his pulling away and coming back. But in adjusting to the ebb and flow of his wandering and restless soul, she had built up defenses, erected walls and wills to protect herself. She needed to be independent, but she also sensed that he couldn't be counted on. She was no longer able to be vulnerable. He alarmed her with threats of suicide. Her defenses flared in response to his pre-occupation with death. She had become more detached, less generous with her compassion. She wondered if he were strengthening her in a peculiar way, preparing her for life without him.

Reflecting, she wondered where their once quintessential passion had flown. What fortunate lovers were enraptured with it now?

2001

SILK OF TENDERNESS

A sweetness pervades,
momentarily erasing loneliness,
and in those dilated moments
my soul finds its mate.

Why doesn't our embrace linger
as it seems to for other lovers
of mutual marrow?

Why do we suffer the silk
of so much tenderness
that we are hung by the knots of it
and made to separate
like convicts sentenced to exile—
even from each other?

Couldn't we hide a little longer
from the gods of pitiless sorrow,
like other smiling lovers?

Is it because the silk of us
is too fine to lie upon?
Is it because our passion
goes far beyond knowing?

Well, I give up any false sense of control
that hangs like an unused leash
around my neck.

It feels tragic—the distance between us,
yet we aren't any more separate now
than when we were together.

Then again, we were
devouring each other like cannibals
and it had to stop.

Perhaps we can keep
re-inventing ourselves,
and transform this tragedy
that gleams for now
like a shattered diamond in the snow.

2009

CHAPTER 2
THE BEAST WITHIN

Captain Voodoo

PRIMORDIAL POWER

Tempests break out
of ancient prisons.

The feral cat's eyes
like terrorized suns
radiate power,
glowing like beacons
trapped in the storm,
piercing the Bible-black night.

A molten savagery
is let to flow
in the gushing stream,
in the leaping river.

The sodden earth sighs,
relieved to be drenched
in something other
than human cruelty.

Once-oppressive heavens
are passive at last,
reposing in the distance.

And the river rises,
enveloping my thighs
as if I'm just another
limb of driftwood.

2005

THE BLACK MIRROR

Marcus does not answer her. He does not listen. Like a black mirror, he emanates narcissism, eating his own tail, seeing only into his own eyes. Call this autism, selfishness, egoism. By any name it's a black mirror—a non-relating, self-orbiting cul-de-sac of tragic isolation.

Like a tree bending over opaque waters, Amy finds no reflection in him. She is thrown back upon herself, forced to be a stranger in a vacuum. Living with Marcus is like living with someone who cannot hear and is emotionally stunted. Art becomes her only soul-mirror, revealing the bare branches of a love-starved tree, but somehow, at the same time, a tree that becomes stronger by relying on itself.

This personal myth also takes expression globally. Non-relating creates poverty, alienation, and intimidation on every level. Call it disembodiment or dissociation, it seems to be another instinctive way to exercise control over others, however unconsciously. Is it genetic? Is it just another facet of nature, like a natural disaster leaving oppression and destruction in its wake? Is it possible consciously to refuse engagement with this self-defeating and isolating mode of behavior? Can such patterns be changed both individually and globally? Or are they simply aspects of nature's chemistry acted out through us?

2004

CARA AND FRAGMENTO
a force propelling a deeper comprehension

There she was again, filled with a curdling kind of compassion, a sympathy that was destroying her. Cara realized she couldn't save her former lover Fragmento from his loneliness and despair. It was painful to be in his presence for long. Having a delicate butterfly-like nature, she tended to absorb his fragmented energy and inevitably became filled with a kind of unconscious dread. Her wings of feelings changed colors with her shifting thoughts and moods.

Why would she be drawn to an energy so oppressive that it could make her suffer, even render her speechless? Did Fragmento represent the alien, dissociated aspect of herself or her family, the shadows yet unrevealed? And why did she have such an extreme capacity for compassion, this compulsion to save exotic and endangered creatures, although it was usually impossible and could actually be detrimental to her?

For some unknown reason, she identified with Fragmento's most grotesque forms of misery. For example, one afternoon when Cara and her lover Pan were out together, Fragmento drove by. Greetings were exchanged, but Cara was left with a sorrowful heart, seeing him so lonely. She knew that he was waiting to visit her as much as possible during his two-week holiday. "What pressure!" Cara complained to Pan, who readily agreed.

Cara felt intimidated by Fragmento's domination and need for control. His drive for power probably came from an inner imbalance, which rendered him continually ill at ease. Overcompensating for a hidden vulnerability, he became all the more aggressive and arrogant towards others.

On the other hand, earlier in their lives together, Fragmento had been her best friend and a gallant hero. He was the muse who had originally ignited her painting. And Fragmento had driven Cara long distances and waited while she spent many precious hours with her father during his last few years. He had been her angel in many ways. They had traveled extensively together and lectured on science and art as a team. But Cara's mind was the antithesis of his, and after three-and-a-half disorienting years together, she felt her mental health threatened by their dissonance and finally demanded that he leave.

Why were these particular dynamics creating such challenges? Perhaps these dynamics were impossible to integrate: oil and water. Or maybe the positive forces were trying to balance the unbalanced. And she was being offered the opportunity to learn more about these energies, about herself in relationship to them. Perhaps, she mused, we unconsciously play out our shadows like puppets on a stage so they can become visible. If we can see through our soul's wounds, perhaps we can begin to heal.

Cara noticed that when she witnessed life from a distance, everything became more clear. To comprehend the seething caldron of life's archetypes was to see deeper into herself, beyond the disguises of personality and cloth. She recognized that her symptoms were both her own and those of the world: the cosmogonic.

And so, as Cara watched Fragmento on his dark blue melancholy drive to the beach, she realized she wasn't willing to join him again in his cul-de-sac of misery.

She remembered how he had wept during a recent dinner together, sentimental about the loss of their intimacy. Oh, how insufferable it was to see him cry. She too had felt disoriented when their passionate bond had first been torn. Feeling thrown off balance, she had stayed away from him for three years in an attempt to regain her equilibrium. Later she continued to try to assist him, and he tried in his own way to help her. But can people really help each other in the ways they intend? Or is growth only possible when people become more aware, grow their own wings, rather than expect another to make up for their limitations? Why bother to go back into the past?

Now, viewing the situation from a more universal perspective, she felt an overwhelming compassion for human suffering. She knew that within the deep well of human cries, within Fragmento, and within herself, were forces propelling an ever-deeper clarity. And she understood that as flowers grow towards the sunlight, so must we all.

1997

CLOSING DOWN THE CIRCUS

I close down tonight's circus.
It is not a success.
The players are weary
and the animals have run away.
The hero has become the antagonist;
the heroine, a clown.
Storms have torn the tent
and the roof leaks.

It is time for the circus to move on.
I have no idea where it will go.
I just know it's over for now.

I turn my back
on the broken violin,
the fallen trapeze,
the humiliation.

And gazing up at an overcast sky,
I remember to disengage
from the phenomena.

2011

EMPTINESS BREEDS INSATIABLE APPETITES

Earlier that day, a flock of humans, resembling hungry birds, ransacked her solitude, her sanctuary. They perched on her pillows and rampaged her living room, requesting food and drink. They came as empty receptacles desperate to be filled with the amenities that only a rich spirit could offer. With their insatiable needs, they ate and drank of both the palpable and the invisible realms for what seemed like forever. When they departed, the priestess, who dwelled there so intimately, was drained. Their rapacious appetites had overwhelmed her. Now she found herself as voracious as they had been—not only for food and drink but also for the unseen.

This hunger, which only growls for more, seems also to propel the camera-clicking, fast-walking tourists visiting the Big Sur wilderness in purposeful frenzy, ravenous for sensory stimulation and instant gratification.

Consumed by these bloodletting ways, she found herself empty.

2002

EXISTENTIAL LONGING

Two black crows and I
gaze out to sea.

What is this existential longing
that haunts my soul,
making me feel
like a tattered flag?

Is it simply part
of the human condition?

After countless days of
battering rain and brutal winds,
at last, the sun appears.

From the confines
of my human cage,
I quietly await
the wingéd exploration of my soul.

Ah, the fragrance
of spring permeates the air.

2010

THE FOOL TO HIS BETRAYER

Fool: Thank you, dear betrayer, for revealing yourself at last. How long I have waited for the scent of your crushed grapes, for only when you are bruised does your true aroma escape.

Betrayer: What on Earth do you speak of? I have no idea!

Fool: You are the predator, donning countless disguises, your rapacious mouth instinctively salivating while another is under duress, especially when there are goods to plunder.

Betrayer: I have always been good and honest, only helping people. How can you concoct such a distortion?

Fool: Because I've suffered from you long enough to study your behaviors, to observe your *modus operandi,* your word foam.

Betrayer: I can't imagine what in the world you are suggesting.

Fool: I have observed how you go for the Achilles heel. You instinctively sniff out a vulnerability and then move in. For instance, vanity is one of your gods, and you use it well to seduce others and later manipulate them.

Betrayer: You make no sense. You hallucinate.

Fool: Once you access a person's vanity, you play up to it until they become enamored and then dependent on the narcotic of your flattery.

Betrayer: I wouldn't lie to anyone; it's the truth of what I feel.

Fool: Perhaps you comprehend so little of who you *really* are that you can't recognize your beast within, or your own hypocrisy. You reek of false virtue. You cajole and prey upon others like a cannibal, then slobber over the picnic.

Betrayer: What foolish drivel. You make no sense whatsoever.

Fool: You entice your prey with promises and services, then eat them silently, without their awareness. Your projections feed their infatuations until it's impossible to know who initiated the process—predator or prey.

Betrayer: Everyone uses projection to exist. Why do you proclaim that my way is treacherous?

Fool: Yours is particularly egregious because you flaunt your so-called consciousness but seem completely unconscious of your shadow side, your savage instincts. You don't just devour your dead prey; you infuse your victims with a false sense of themselves through your pretentious flattery, then silently suck their blood. You live off their vanity-fed realities.

Betrayer: It all sounds grotesque, these delusions of yours. How do you know this isn't really you, not me at all?

Fool: I know because of the toxicity you leave in your wake. You create unnecessary toil for others, confusion and chaos. It's easy to know someone by what surrounds them, and the trail of their effects. And you reveal your emptiness of seed in your barren garden, in your anemic daughter who lives through you, whom you lord over and thus enslave. You are the feral animal in frantic pursuit of fresh sustenance. You compliment first, breaking the skin of the grape, then you drink the wine of your kill. As usual, the micro is mirrored in the macro. Your plight is no different from the world's. You suffer from myopia of the psyche, presenting a sincere and congenial mask, but feigning ignorance of your hidden savagery.

2004

AT BUENA GARDENS, SAN FRANCISCO

Inscribed in white marble under the elegant fountains at Buena Gardens is the heroic credo of Dr. Martin Luther King. In contrast, my own view of the world has become soberingly realistic and at odds with his lofty sentiments. To speak of justice and equality for all is of course preferable but utterly illusionary and based on ideals that have never yielded those realities.

As one walks the streets of San Francisco, there is no evidence of equality or justice for all. Nor are there many examples of this anywhere in our barbaric, war-driven world. The blood of man is pulsing with conflict, chaos, and derision. Of course there are individual exceptions, and we must always navigate towards our highest potential, regardless. But war is in the very bloodstream of the human animal and always has been. Can that biological fact be changed by our idealistic projections?

Our biology is compelled to produce whatever neuro-transmitters and peptides we require.[2] We live and act out of necessity to fulfill our sometimes angelic and other times monstrous systems. The basis of who we are is biological, and this determines much of our behavior and motivation. Our emotions and spirituality are the voices of our bodies. Swedenborg says, "We swim towards our food."

When guided by awareness, we can climb the spiral from raw instinct and bestiality to the tower of song.[3] This is possible for the individual—but remains highly questionable for the masses.

2007

THE BOARD OF DOGS

The calamity had reached epidemic proportions. Because of their severe overpopulation problem, humans were being caged and carried into hospitals for spaying and neutering by their dog-masters. Ever-accelerating violence was erupting into bloodbaths across the planet.

At one such hospital, Chico, the Mongrel, director of the board of dogs, had called an emergency meeting to address this alarming situation. Quickly, the board members had assembled. Chico opened the meeting with a rather grave declaration:

"Humans have proved themselves treacherous, having acted out their rabid instincts in vulgar and ominous ways. They are the most endangered species, due to their insistence on self-annihilation. They have not evolved beyond their survival instincts[4] with their so-called consciousness. At least a dog is a dog and doesn't feign enlightenment, altruism, virtue, and all the other righteous façades."

Clarissa, the Dalai Afghan, secretary to the director, responded in a contemplative tone:

"You would think that, if humans had their basic needs met, they could live from awareness, with consideration for their fellow men. But obviously this is not the case. When survival emotions are ignited, consciousness vanishes; the will to power[5] and other voracious instincts, such as rivalry, greed, and territorialism, reign with insatiable appetite. Even someone with extensive spiritual cultivation may still revert to savagery, however subtly disguised, if these rudimentary instincts are aroused. The philosopher-sage who lives on a mountaintop can quickly descend to the survival level if he feels threatened."

Then Dr. Wanda, the Whippet Hound, regional advisor for those hospitals overseeing the spaying and neutering of humans, barked in a steady staccato proclaiming:

"We live on a precarious brink between life and death. We all know that without our survival instincts we die; so in a way these instincts could be regarded as our ultimate saviors. On the other hand, these primal impulses, which are fueled by the polarities, often seem to be running the world through us. Yet people think *they* are in command. How ludicrous," the Whippet yipped shrilly. "No wonder people are driven by fear. They have little control over their instincts, especially when they feel threatened. When acting from a state of agitation and fear, they only perpetuate their defensive posture, but they are usually the last ones to recognize this."

"How can our consciousness liberate us if ultimately the survival bullies are in charge? Are we doomed?" grunted Chico, the Mongrel, the sturdy spokes-dog. Licking his white, pointed fangs with a healthy, pink tongue, he continued, "I don't think so. But we need to study humans, lest we become like them. By understanding and accepting the eternal laws, we will better comprehend how the universe works through us, and perhaps we can learn to navigate our instincts with higher intention, at least more often."

"It is a human-eat-human world," retorted Wanda the Whippet with her narrow, pointed countenance. "As dogs, we are well aware of the world's food chain and how every living creature must eat other life-forms to survive. Beyond the known predators, our food chain also includes germs, bacteria, every kind of stress, and countless other hidden energy vampires. We need to recognize this earthly condition, its symptoms, and whenever possible, spiritualize our instincts. Whether we are born tyrants or victims, the predator-prey forces are fueling us. Since our survival instincts signal imminent danger or safety, they provide the underlying neuronal network for our continued existence. This recognition of how we are wired is essential if we are to rise above our present primitive bestiality."

These observations prompted Bernice, a matronly Saint Bernard, to share a disturbing experience she recently had with one of her grown offspring. With consternation, she recounted how her son Octavio exhibited rage and territorialism when he felt disempowered. Bernice concluded that his insufferable behavior was symptomatic of an inability to maintain a higher consciousness in the face of primitive impulses. She knew from her study of psychology that the subliminal desire of offspring to eat and possess the mother was survival-based and ignited by a sense of insecurity and lack of control. Yet all the basic necessities had been provided for Octavio: love, food, shelter, and spiritual guidance. Even so, the higher awareness of this usually mature dog had apparently been overwhelmed by instinctive biological urges. And at the time, Bernice herself, feeling abandoned by Octavio, had descended to the level of base impulses.

"Here we see examples," Clarissa summarized, "of consciousness being tyrannized by survival instincts, as if an embrace of higher principles had never existed."

In a penetrating voice, Chico barked rapidly, overriding Bernice's maternal laments. "These primitive forces are also the underlying dynamics propelling the world's grist of challenges, like volcanoes or hurricanes spewing out of Mother Earth with a kind of vengeance. The Earth's soul is being pillaged and raped by the patriarchal systems." With a penetrating voice, he continued: "These same behaviors are being acted out in myriad ways within the familial dynamics of innumerable living creatures. It's obvious that territorialism and predator-prey syndromes run the zoo! The need to eat goes way beyond just its literal interpretation. Power and greed can be thought of as defense systems fueled by fear and expressed as exaggerated needs for self-preservation. Apparently these instincts are at the very root of civilization, ruling our lives, running our planet. If this were not the case, the miracle we know as Life could not exist."

Spontaneously and with a gentle intensity, Clarissa, the Dalai Afghan, added: "Our instincts parade like wild beasts in our psyche's jungles, unbeknownst to ourselves, in the primitive rituals of self-sacrifice and the endless bloodbaths of wars." Suddenly introspective, the Afghan priestess looked down and murmured, "Ah, this insight is a divine gift from the gods, a blessing born of our suffering, the radiance which suffuses the dark with light. I feel compelled to re-seminate these golden seeds of revelation," she exclaimed ecstatically. (The golden hound was both a university professor and renowned poet.)

Then Ralph, the Standard Poodle, a more domesticated dog, mentioned how the three feral cats living with him exhibit the same will to power, territorialism, and competition, as is the case for all creatures struggling to survive. "The father cat is the tough one," he pointed out, "chasing away his own children to dominate his domain and ensure food for himself first."

Bernice, the St. Bernard, chuckled from the folds of her meaty jowls and mumbled under her breath, "I could learn from that feral cat."

"Perhaps we can use our consciousness to navigate our instincts when we are not in survival mode," yapped Dr. Wanda, raising her tawny eyebrows and putting her glasses on the table. "Yet," she continued wearily, "awareness is not its own redemption; one can still be ruled by the rudimentary when fear is encountered. And obviously it is essential that it be this way for survival. I agree that we can let our noble passions transform us, using ourselves and the media of life as our crucible," she added with an ebullient burst of passion.

"Evolution is just a biased perspective or false hope," snarled Xavier, the Pit Bull, who had been listening with bared teeth behind a forced grin. "Don't go into the arena with the devil, meaning anyone or any thought that condemns the mind to futility, that inflames the soul to suffering. You will just be ground like hamburger to feed the Insatiable Monster," he growled.

"The alternative," chanted Clarissa, the Dalai Afghan, "is to re-alchemize our suffering through art and other expressions of higher intention. In this way, our experience becomes a means of comprehending life's dynamics and transposing them, thus infusing our creations with spirit and understanding. In this sense, our art forms embody our assimilated life ingredients."

"How visceral and cannibalistic," the Pit Bull interjected with another aggressive yelp. "But that's life on Earth," he added with a slobbering sneer.

Then Wanda, the Whippet Hound, shook her tawny, pointed ears and emphatically proclaimed, "May we serve the gods that be, the creators or destroyers who are forever feasting and digesting us, employing us for their dung. Nevertheless, we know that good and evil are both acts of the gods—organic necessities—like them or not. It's the consciousness we bring to them that may make a difference." Her steady brown eyes directly met the sober gaze of the other board members.

With fur bristling, Chico, the Mongrel, who was eager to summarize, muttered dog-matically: "Higher vision can only come when humans feel safe, which is not always possible. It's interesting to notice how people and countries often evolve in a parallel fashion. In undeveloped countries, where the basic needs of countless people go unmet, oppression rules and desires often turn murderous. On the other paw, when humans become too complacent or bourgeois, a decline sets in. So it appears that survival instincts, if guided by our awareness, can provide the trampoline for transcendence. Without this possibility, human beings merely exist as automatons at the mercy of their appetites and fears, the tyranny of our socio-economic systems."

"Yet if we live as monks from the higher mind, aren't we still prey to other perhaps unseen predators?" interjected Ralph, the Standard Poodle. "Clearly, the forces of nature in their innumerable masks orchestrate the miracle of existence and the balancing act of the opposites. So perhaps evolution is merely a concept for optimists who need the insulin of theoretical belief systems."

At this point, weary of the discussion, all the dogs on the board agreed to howl their closing statement in unison: "Let us be brave about this wild stallion called Life and look ever higher to the eternal spirit behind our mortal follies."

"End of meeting!" Chico announced abruptly, his black eyes looking rather bloodshot.

And a caged human could be heard mumbling from the hall, "It really is a dog-eat-dog world—only we exist more like dogs than they do."

Nearby, another human behind bars responded, "Yes, the dogs really *have* taken over. Perhaps they will do a better job than we have!"

After they had left their board meeting, the dogs agreed that if humans could ever spiritualize their instincts, they would let them out of their cages.

2003

A TUG FROM THE SUBTERRANEAN

An erosive complacency
wears on my bones,
devouring my marrow
with an uncaring hunger,
sinking my roots into quicksand.

As I descend deeper
into the fleshy arms of lassitude,
I try to think of this deathly tug
as merely a kind of rest.

But something else,
perhaps ominous, perhaps benign,
is speaking to me
in an unfamiliar tongue.

I sense that this tug
is from the subterranean,
from an ancient primal order—
a code that could reveal
more of the mystery
of being human, of being alive
in this stifling way.

Then, at last, my soul
emerges from the shadows,
through the Daemon's flame.

2009

BLACK PANTHER ON A LEASH

I observe myself drifting to the surface of my cerebral aquarium as I wait impatiently for fresh images to shake themselves free of their embryonic disguises.

Which archetypal force will emerge like a crashing ocean wave? What form will appear as the next chimera, expressing what instincts, breathing through which nostrils of bird, beast, or human?

I draw curtains of analytical conjecture across this stage of my shuddering shoulders. Threatening forces of the future have already punctured my diaphanous being with coarse, muffled tones.

Isn't awareness supposed to be the liberator of suffering? And what exactly is the price paid for the mind's intervention? When the analytical mind is called in, I feel depersonalized, almost disembodied. I temporarily hang from the gallows and lose my sublime intuition. Why isn't higher intention enough to seminate the rough cobblestone path of life with a friendly moss?

Is it because we don't choose the spume of our spray, the archetypal forces that mold our clay? Speaking as a world-stranger, it appears that a sticky narcissism prompts us to think we have freedom of will, that we choose our own light or dark lords—yet the miracle of life comes without our will and blows its horn through our particular and diverse instruments from an uncanny intelligence, at random, the sublime in undesign. The stream of consciousness engendered by the poetic gods seems to flow back to the infinite seas when survival instincts begin their somersaults and their militant performance of duty in defense.

You, dear Reader, may say, "Well, so what if we don't have destiny tightly bridled? And so what if we temporarily exchange our primal connectedness for a metallic plate of fear-driven analysis?"

For me, this purging of my soul demands the poet's pen, the artist's paint. As a mock-human, I find salvation in splattering the guts of these fleshy thoughts upon the page or canvas in a kind of bulimic splendor. And perhaps one day, other explorers wandering the offbeat alleys of peculiar and revealing inner realms will discover these words and images anew.

This self-seized pondering was interrupted when a youthful, seemingly innocent male knocked on my front door. Unabashedly, without even introducing himself, this stranger asked whether I would consent to keep on my property, on a long leash, a magnificent, shiny, black panther. The young man added that this animal had been with him since childhood and was quite well trained, although it was necessary to take certain precautions. He gave cause to his request, stating that my spacious and quiet land was the perfect property for this animal.

Presumptuously, he explained that as long as the panther was leashed, he would not be in my way. All I needed to do, he mentioned casually, was to throw any living creature in the panther's radius and he would kill it immediately. Then the curly-blond-headed youth naively added, "If there aren't any mice in your mouse traps or extra kittens or stray cats, you can always feed him horsemeat or canned dog-food." And as if that weren't audacious enough of this impetuous intruder, he continued: "Sometimes, letting him go hungry won't hurt him, but on the days he fasts, be careful not to get too close to him." With this last horrific comment, he put his hands in his pockets and peered at me with the dazed, faraway gaze of an imbecile.

"Why in the world would you presume that I would even consider keeping a dangerous blood-thirsty beast here?" I angrily retorted, rather shocked by his invasive appearance and request.

"Why not?" he questioned. "How is a leashed panther who exhibits who he is and what he needs different from all the people who come here without leashes to restrain their instincts?"

After these last rather alarming remarks, he began whistling to himself, then abruptly and wordlessly walked away. And I was left with this somewhat carnal tale, only partially digested.

Later, I realized I had spilt vermillion-colored ink on the white tablecloth of pretension. And now, dear Reader, I throw the meatless bone of discomfort to you to bury.

After experiencing and observing numerous cat and mouse sacrifices, I understand how essential they are in fueling the next creation. And thus, I acknowledge the black panther within us all.

2003

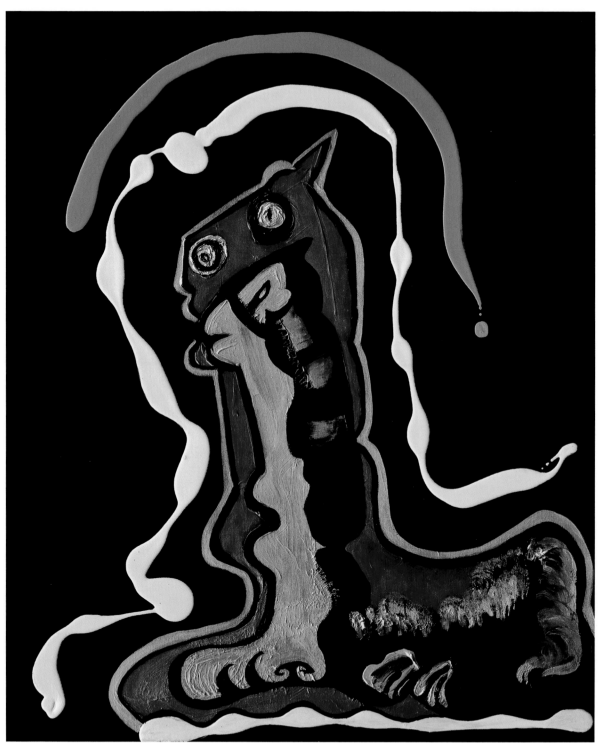

Needja, the Young Cat

IN PRAISE OF THE FERAL

Miranda was an unusual deer in that she preferred a reclusive existence, except for the company of a few unique friends, and certainly never hind-leggers.

Her friends included a wild female cat whose gold eyes were filled with the fear of living in the wilderness. Miranda loved this spooked-out, black-and-white creature. She also counted as a friend the male feral cat, more black than white, who was heard mating with the female last night to moaning shrieks.

Somehow when Miranda gazed into the honest, untamed eyes of the mangy girl cat, she felt her own panic about existence. And when she gazed into the eyes of the black-and-white furred male cat, she felt his power from having survived in the wilds. She also felt an honesty, a directness that human eyes seldom revealed. It was easier to look into their wild gold eyes than into humans' busy, used-up eyes that didn't reflect back their souls. She liked creatures that were simple and honest about who they really were. She was tired of city cats and people-poodles.

She had heard that the human-beasts had been murdering each other for eons in efforts to control their territory. In fact, they had shot and murdered members of her own family high up in the mountains. Did they regard the land they so coveted as an extension of their own bodies? She knew that territorialism was a powerful instinct. It could make even tame creatures kill each other to enforce their own boundaries. But was that enough to explain their savage impulses, she wondered, wiggling her moist, brown muzzle.

Miranda was relieved she didn't need to erect fences or put up signs. Where she lived, clear, fresh streams assuaged her thirst, and endlessly rolling mountains and meadows stretched out to roam. Unlike the hind-leggers, she didn't own anything or need to. She was self-sufficient. She had fur to keep her warm in the winter and a remarkable ability to leap and run unlike any leashed-up human homeowner. The wilderness opened its heart to this wild creature. Both the beams of the stars and the rays of the sun dappled her fur and sung her soul.

Her requirements were basic. What a great turn of fate to be born a deer and not a human who needs to possess and control things, she mused.

2003

REQUIEM FOR CAGED BIRDS

O pale, wan bird, lost from the sun, imprisoned behind the steel bars of a sterile cage, neither leaves nor branches line your impoverished cell. And no feathered companion greets you; only a tiny mirror stares vacantly into your betrayed existence. The sun rises and flowers near your prison, but no one notices that you are withering in the shade, and no one moves you to the light. You are left without the gold of the sun's warmth to green your graying feathers.

Do those who ignorantly stole your birthright live the same way, clipping their wings as they have clipped yours?

Outside, the cawing of bluebirds mingles with other untamed songs.

O, impoverished little creature, forsaken to the avarice of commercialism, in your dreams do you join your kin soaring in the heavens? How long has your sunless heart been broken from flight?

If your captor suddenly opened the door of your cage, would you even recognize the chance to recapture your wingéd glory?

2004

AS IF IN A TRANCE

The tiny cries of a tree
bending in the breeze
sound like a baby
being born from wonder
in the darkness of love,
hidden now in
the infinities, whispering.

Not hearing
this lullaby of subtle whimpers
in the ebony well of night,
the waves continue searching the sands
and the sea churns on.

And we, like circus animals,
even if the stars fall at our feet,
keep jumping through
our self-made hoops,
as if in a life-long trance.

2011

CHAPTER 3
HOMAGE TO SILENCE

Quantum Diva

I HEAR YOU LISTENING
for David

Ah, I hear you listening,
sounding soft, receptive of love,
like the dawn's first light
complexioning the mountain shoulders.

I hear you listening
like the spume of the wind
racing across the sea,
like the dove above, in silent flight.

I hear you listening
like an anointed orchard,
ripening fragrant in the summer's heat.

Ah, you offer your listening
like a pearlescent cape,
comforting my heart.

2010

BATHING IN SILENCE

Feeling invisible, I wander into the pervading stillness enshrouding my home, breathing deeply of its balm. I wonder if Silence notices me. My edges soften gradually into a delicate silk, and I feel Silence smiling at me as I blossom in this meadow of quietude.

Having bathed in this beloved realm, I am no longer the raw-edged human who first entered. Eventually, I stumble out of my invisibility as one drifting out of a dream, emerging from a translucent, infinite pool, my senses vibrant and renewed. And I return to the earthly realms—resplendent.

2008

FURTHER RUMINATIONS

Splendorous radiance floods the Ventana Mountains. Robed within by the sun-drunk moments, we imbibe the ambrosia of verdant forests nearby.

We find a garden refuge high up at the Ventana Inn where dappled sunlight dances upon lush plants and flowers. The sea below is mute and calm in the sun's blanching valor.

The sudden appearance of a lizard diverts my attention from writing. Curious to see how he will respond, I pour water into a groove near him on a wooden bench, but he makes no move. I observe that his tail is longer than the rest of him. What kind of lizard is he, I wonder.

The lizard hardly stirs and displays no interest in the water. Obviously, I am the thirsty one. The tourist traffic on Highway One drones on below like a computer game. Blue jays caw in the trees surrounding me as I return to my journal-writing. While my blood turns to ink upon the page, the shadow cast by my pale, blue-veined hand seems to smirk at my impermanence. Ah, at last the lizard inches forward.

At that moment, I stand up and speak briefly to my companion. He complains that he can't work because of my interruptions. He is surrounded by piles of crumpled drawings. As I turn away from him, I continue to eye the lizard, who now appears tempted by the water. Patiently I wait, a predator of observation, the quasi-scientist. He has his back to me, its primal designs so displayed.

I find another sequestered nook close by and continue to write, my shadow faithfully following my hand across the page. Meanwhile, in the boundless spheres, the sun's blood-fire laughs with freedom as it races breathlessly ahead of the twilight.

When I leave this nook of reflection, a tourist asks me, "What is it like down there?"

"Enchanting," I murmur.

Continuing with the experiment, I add more water to another tiny groove in the rustic bench. I glance back at the lizard who has now turned directly toward the water, still not taking a sip. What does this mean? I chuckle to myself, bending down to meet the eyes of my primordial playmate.

Finally ready to depart, I feel a strange sense of satisfaction with this unfinished experiment, grateful for this unrushed quality of experience, this time in the timeless.

2004

ROYAL EXILE

Freezing sheets of rain thrash the little redwood cabin perched upon the mountaintop. All of life brings itself to this citadel amidst the starry heavens.

Nearby, herds of deer munch with delicate hesitancy on the lush winter grass where hungry mountain lions lurk in wait. As the snow spreads its white cloaks over the high steeples of the Ventana mountains, a coyote drags a rat out of its burrow, gobbling it whole. The orchids in our winter haven plead for sunlight after the raging storms.

Every form of life in this vast wilderness offers a unique voice. We poets express innermost replicas of the surrounding wilderness in our art, each with a unique interpretation, following sublime intuition, being receptive to Otherness.

Retreat feels like our most sublime choice. Living in simplicity, synchronicity, spontaneity regenerates us. Hunger for quietude is the primary urge and Taoistic meditation, our most nourishing sustenance. To live here is to be in royal exile.

This solitary refuge upon the mountain peak has endured for over thirty years, holding its own, unmarred by the blasting winds and merciless tempests. Through the accumulation of solitude within its walls, this simple temple with its high-beamed ceilings pulses with character. Myriad windows open to new panoramas of perception; we behold the raw wilderness in all its enigmatic splendor. Here, fog entities ebb and flow, re-shaping colossal mountains, moistening patient forests, the tiniest flowers.

We observe that each element contains every other, the fog, thunder, lightning, storms, winds, sun and moon, the rocks and seas below, stars above; nothing breathes separately. And each makes its own unique contribution. So it appears that even the most pathetic and dense of human spirits, seemingly birthed at random by Nature, are essential to existence. Realizing this inspires the patience of a vulture and the distant vision of an eagle.

This land we are rooted in mirrors our own energies. We experience the natural world around us through the instruments of our beings; the meanings we glean are of the soul. Our art reveals that everything is an essential ingredient and that the laws that apply to the physical universe apply to the soul's wilderness as well.

Within the polarities of universal forces, contrasts inhabit us all: peace and violence, beauty and ugliness, love and betrayal. We remember to celebrate every aspect of creation, even despair, as essential grist for the spiritual mill.[6]

2001

HERE I FIND YOU

I find you in the yearning,
in the last plea of twilight,
in the darkening silhouettes of trees,
in the seemliness of things.

As the quietude unfolds
within the somber, settling house,
redwood walls lose their ghosts.
For the moment, only silence
inhabits the dusky sea.

And here in the seed
you dwell, in all faces, no faces,
in the enveloping darkness expanding,
pulsing with life—
yet beyond this, in the nothingness,
in the blue well of silence,
in the stillness of eternal communion.

2011

THE MONKS AT THE BOWERBIRD NEST

The Bowerbird Nest[7] is a small redwood cabin perched high above the sea and the village of Big Sur. This human roost is set in bedrock amidst white limestone slabs, close to the nests of eagles, hawks, and falcons. Built for survival like a tough little beast, this redwood cabin in the wilderness nobly bears the most brutal of winter storms.

To enter this silent sanctuary is to enter another resonance. It seems possessed by the spirits of ancient monks and the demands they make of us if we are to live here in cadence with the Mystery. A mystic, religious tone, both austere and lyrical, pervades. In the pink candlelight, the wood panels of this cozy habitat glow with an insistent pulse. Any sound is invasive when basking in this great reservoir of accumulated silence. Here, we are instantly transported beyond time.

Myriad windows of cosmic eyes offer enigmatic panoramas of beauty, views into more universal perspectives. With such vastness beheld, we synthesize the finite with the infinite and find ourselves in continuous transition. We behold nature's wonders through every sense, not just our eyes.

And what do the monks utter through the redwood walls, and what do they lament? They seem insistently to request silence, simplicity, the shedding of labors bred by stale habit or willfulness, urging us instead toward effortless creation. In this way, as poets open to life's flow, we are continually dissolving fabrications and renewing our souls.

The long, vertical window in the living room with its tall cross of wooden beams forms a crucifix, symbolizing the metamorphosis required to birth jewels of the spirit. This is not only for poets in the process of creating but also for all evolving souls.

Yes, the monks request a reverence towards all of life—the tiniest wildflower's heart, the wandering clouds in billowy drift, the sheen of dawn's rays illuminating the mountain shoulders. They ask that we move in harmony with the elemental rhythms, that we see the world as the coyote or deer, that we observe the flux of all rhythms as one. The junco birds with their tiny black beaks hunt for seeds, spontaneously flying away like musical chords. The dew-embroidered leaves and the emerald, glistening grasses all are revered. The monks are quietly grateful that we are silent and listening.

We dwell within the monks' seed of murmuring, in the sacred, ceaseless flame of creation. Our urge sings of the need to empty ourselves as much as possible of the density of today's noisy distractions that numb the higher resonance. We are constantly called to shed the moment's garb, to penetrate beneath the surface of things. When we do, we discover the timeless in time, and hear the lost notes of the cosmic symphony, the origins reborn in every moment.

We let our sensibilities flourish in the wilderness, verdant sprouts of a perennial spring. We thrive within the raindrops' crystalline worlds, allowing our hidden seeds to be dormant until their next faces are revealed. We live in a Taoistic dance that lets the birthing process be in its many cycles, trusting the enigmatic hand of nature as a guiding muse. Knowing that nothing is insignificant, we live in a continual state of alertness, letting the synchronistic wonders of life's manifestations mirror our own myths. Having a silent rapport with each other, we are in attunement as chords in the infinite symphony. In this continuum of meditations, we weave our inner threads of revelation into the outer worlds, translating our poetic passion into art, casting our richly embroidered threads into the Cosmic Loom.

These walls ask us, as the monks do, to be male of womb, feminine inside the masculine. They encourage us to be protean, brave of spirit in facing the inevitable cycles of death and rebirth, devoted to the untamed music that ignites our souls.

The monks are invisibly part of these natural wonders. Wilderness offers us its breath without the imposition of human will. A continuous prayer emanates from this luxurious bed of quietude, these ancient ways bred from reservoirs of solitude.

With this mystic weaving underlying our flame's urge, we live the life the monks didn't allow themselves, the whimsy and chance of the moment, the effortless movement of our tides upon uncharted shores.

Now, the crystalline air drifts in through our windows from the firstborn breaths of snow capping the peaks of the surrounding Ventana mountains. The pristine air imbibes our passion, reverberating with the pulse of infinity. Flames roaring in the hearth beat their drums in testament to our re-found grace; blazing logs carry the blood of the redwoods' sacrifice.

The candles seem to thrive on the erotic love we breed in this temple, born of that luxurious Otherness. The burgundy-colored carpets bleed of our royal glow. This outwardly primitive nest, lavish on the inside, is feathered with our spirits' plumage.

This is some of what the monks lamented but which now is ours, woven from our passion. And they welcome into their austere cells and caves of longing our offering that had previously eluded them, letting us fill their once-empty vases with an extravagance of fragrant wildflowers.

2001

A FOREST NEARBY

The woodland,
deep and still,
holds reservoirs of silence
without thought or plan.

Primal wells quench
the thirsting roots
searching for origin
in mindless motion.

Stillness can be felt
by listening deeply;
the repose of pulse
almost quivers.

Who else comes to this forest
besides the grazing deer
and warbling bird?

Here, neglect reigns as virtue
in the forgotten tangle of limbs,
wreathed with abandon,
obscuring the fence of purpose.

2005

A REALM BIRTHED IN SILENCE

for Benedict de Spinoza

My home luxuriates in silence. I gaze through the myriad open doors, and other realms gaze back. I imagine our planet without human corruption for these moments in darkness, in the timeless. Our world at once becomes an empty canvas from which to create. All the conditioning appears as pollution of our endless projections and prejudice—self-made cages suffocating the inner almond tree in blossom.

For these moments, I bathe in this unconditioned realm of sheer possibility. I cast off the extraneous, ready for liberation, for fresh landscapes. As the numinous silently beams from the darkness, I humbly begin again.

2007

HEAVEN'S MIST

Enshrouded in winter's skin,
wearing it inside out,
she walks about
white and vapory
like heaven's mist.

With her sister, the fog,
she lies snug in vagary.
Fed from silence,
she has no mouth,
preferring the arcs of quiet.

She lives upon a mountaintop
and slithers to a nearby lagoon
where, as an ethereal water nymph,
she swims the primal waters,
imbibing the briny breath
of the seas below.

There is no gravity
in those waters—
her vapor mirrors
the clouds above.

Yes, this is what winter is for,
she muses, to be wrapped
in Nature's robes
rather than the coarse fiber
of cacophonous crowds.

2009

THE THIRST FOR METAMORPHOSIS

It felt like ages since they had inhabited this realm, this world above the others. Here, stillness answered them in lyrical rhythms, resonating with the surrounding wilderness.

Fenced in only by her own stories, Eden reclined in a comfortable chair, editing the written expressions of her wild imagination. Fidel played the organ of his heart, the guitar, his music mirroring the soul of the wild meadows they perched upon, hundreds of feet above the sea and the small village of Big Sur. Fog had blanketed most of the town and forests below. The cars and trucks on Highway One, appearing like mechanical toys, zoomed ahead, buzzing like the territorial wood bees around them.

Fidel remarked that the human mind can never really be quiet, that even the monk is in dialogue, bringing his own god for company.

But despite the mind's need for a sense of progress, they both felt silently enriched from being in the stillness, amidst such expansive vistas.

When it was time in the timeless to depart, a gigantic beetle suddenly landed in Eden's lap as if hurled from above. It was a reddish-brown insect with six jagged legs, long antennae, and large black eyes. Startled, she leapt up, scratching the skin on her right arm near the elbow. When Fidel saw that her arm was bleeding, he kissed and licked the wound, proclaiming that now they were linked incestuously, of the same blood.

Later, she reflected on the symbolic significance of this event. Curiously, on Fidel's recommendation she had just purchased a collection of Kafka's short stories, which she had been eager to read. So, when Fidel suggested that the beetle could be a message from Kafka, her curiosity was aroused, and she began reading the collection that very evening.

A few days later, inspired by Kafka and the book's introduction by Joyce Carol Oates, an exciting new story began to weave its way through Eden. It was as if the synchronicity of incidents was divinely orchestrated to draw her attention within, in a will-less, predestined way, as if she were living time backwards and into the future simultaneously.

As Eden continued to ponder these unusual occurrences, she recognized her need to reconnect with the silence that revealed her soul. It was this urge that had brought them to the mountaintop. But with this desire also came a cry, a ravaging thirst for metamorphosis which mysteriously had manifested in the appearance of the enormous beetle.

2003

SILENCE AND ITS PARADOXES

I rest on a rotting log in a secluded nook I named "The Tree Cemetery." I'm drawn here because it is usually quiet, although now the airwaves carry jeers of baseball players and barks of dogs. Fortunately the autumnal music of a nearby river cascades over the stones, transcending all other sounds.

Is my continuous yearning for quietude a symbol of being drawn to the Void? If so, how voluptuously contradictory it is that this urge tends to spawn its opposite. The wilderness of the unconscious offers infinite travel without requiring passports or baggage. The eternal roots of being are expanded in *not doing*. In that lush emptiness comes the opportunity to die to the moment and be reborn from the womb of the invisible. As Spinoza said, "In turning away from life, I have life." Or as Saltus suggested, "In not wanting, I have." And on and on the contradictions raise their mocking chimeras, masks disguising underlying, unseen forces.

Ah yes, and when the compulsion of day is obliterated by the benevolence of night's ebony seeds, so is the sun's insolence.

Again the contrasts proudly parade their palette, light to dark, sun to moon, birth to death. Silence, an anonymous and infinite reservoir, patiently awaits. Only by dying to life, spurning its appetites and desires, do we discover a portal of calm underlying the chaos of today's world. In that dissolving into emptiness, memory becomes a faded servant of the hopeless, and our spirits are revivified.

Are we capable of fasting in reverence, letting go of the mind's gymnastics, feeding on the glory of nothingness, reveling in its languor? What then, but wonder at that which emanates from this fecund well of being? The word *sacred* is often used these days, but isn't it a twin to *silence?*

Quality experience requires that our senses be acute, awake in the moment. Yet how over-input-ed our wild goats of the senses[8] have become. Can the subtle and poetic survive? Compulsive and mechanical behaviors, born of anxiety, seem to ravage the breath of wonder. But are any of us immune from robotic behavior? Ironically, even peaceniks can be as militant and fierce in their drives as warmongers, and therefore just as noisy and insensitive.

And there I go, spouting off about all the cacophony in the world as I sit on a dead log writing notes about silence. What absurd ironies inhabit me.

If I could visualize silence, how would it appear? As a hesitant meadow of white daisies in the Bible-black night? Or as an enchanted forest of slumbering redwoods? Or would it be like dreaming without a dream?

2004
at the Big Sur Lodge

IN THE STILLNESS

Laughing with beneficence,
the sun floods light again
on this paradise.
And flowers sip the beams.

I wander like a ghost
through these sacred gardens,
observing my solitude.
The flowers don't seem to mind.

Another poet wanders nearby,
sunk in his own sensibilities.

Artists need this realm
outside of time
to dive for their treasures.

I retreat into nothingness . . .
and the haunting questions
dissolve in the stillness.

2006

THE FOOL AND THE BLUE JAY

At a nearby inn, high up in a garden Eden, I find a dusty plank of wood to rest upon. Here I can dream, in the hidden white light where no one can peer upon my diaphanous spirit realm. This open temple without walls is infinite in soul, like the seas below.

Gazing at the summer's weary dust, I feel the triumph of escaping the Monday machine, the maintenance realm called reality. To fully enjoy an inspiring quality of life, I attempt to avoid the militant mode. My way of experiencing life's ambrosia is to renounce the very things that most people crave.

I savor every beam of the sun's persistence as it stares through a silhouette of trees. The monsters of the economic grid turn their heads to ignore my escape as I continue to breathe in the ephemeral sweetness enveloping me.

These molecular moments wait like thirsty birds for a drink of spirit water. The languor of my longing awaits intoxication, like an unseen meadow longing to be filled with golden beams of the sun.

In living the moment with such ardor, the blue jay overhead seems to mirror my inner muse. He apparently thrives without a self-centered psyche. His wings are real, unlike my invisible ones; so is his flight. As he soars, he chirps, "Watch me; I am Is-ness."

Meanwhile, as a human, bound by my ribcage, I await deliverance for flight. I continue to reflect on the contradictions that fuel the polarities that give breath to life, bringing form to the formless, light to the dark, infinity to the finites. Through the contrasts, possibility breathes. Because of paradox, we exist. The yin-yang of the polarities swings the pendulum, making life possible.

Here in this garden sanctuary, I feel carefree, open to exploring the unfamiliar. Wilderness offers me an empty page for my imagination to take flight—experiment. The sun's warmth caresses my head as if to reassure me that I have my guardians and that I will live on, for now.

Suddenly the silence is wounded by the crunch of gravel. I glance to the gardens above. Fortunately, the footsteps quickly vanish. And I continue to write quietly in my journal, like a nanny goat busily devouring paper, undisturbed on this oceanic day while the blue jay's caw mocks my ponderings.

2004
in the herb garden at the Ventana Inn

THE GRACE OF QUIETUDE

In a lavender twilight,
the dew of the formless emerges,
soon to be enshrouded
by an ebony night.

No sound is formed by lips,
just the soothing grace of quietude.

Invisible realms, waiting
in the timeless, encompass me.

Energy fields, accessible only in silence,
visit me behind the veils, freed now
from human concept.

These ever-expanding worlds,
arising from the primal oceans,
come without cost.

As a Taoist,
explorer of unseen treasures,
I revel in these sacred gems.

2011

CHAPTER 4
PARADOXICAL POSES

The Fierce Wills of the Dark Bird and Lady

SEASONS OF THE GODS

The seasons of the gods
pulse through us—
a paradoxical pageant.

Yes, an unsung melody
sings us indifferently,
while the neck bone of Paradox
pulls us through
the eye of its needle.

One moment . . .
rainbows arch the skies.
And red tulips sprout before spring.

The next . . .
illusion devours us,
abandoning our orange peels
on alien desert sands.

In the midst of this chaos,
we stop and question
what we are doing.

What is all this?
The phantasmagoric spectacle
called Life.

2007

LARA AND RAOUL

Resting in the lush, sun-filled aviary, listening to the fountain's lyrical waters splashing over mossy stones, Lara reflected on the day.

The night before had been so ragged that she lay awake wondering if death were imminent. Her nerves had been frayed by the world's rattle. Yet the day had miraculously turned out to be exactly what she needed. Withdrawing at the eleventh hour of fragility's scream, she had wandered down a sea-path by the wild forest of redwoods to her poet-lover's cabin. He was sleeping when she arrived, so she reclined outside and waited as the sun's radiance rose and fell behind the billowy, drifting clouds.

Somehow her sacred instincts guided her to what she needed most. And somehow Raoul knew that, as a poet, perhaps he needed the same thing. They had been each other's spirit-light for years before they met, writing to each other from far away, Raoul from the valley, Lara from the cliffs above the sea. Then he had moved into her nearby cabin, and they began to know the embodied aspects of each other. Since then, they had alchemized the joys and challenges that the forces of nature had channeled like wind currents through them.

Lara had arrived at Raoul's cabin like a tiny, starving bird, her ancient soul shrunk in grief, dissolved into ashes. Having allowed her gifts to become weapons, she now beheld the horror of their loss. Then, when Raoul awoke and read Robinson Jeffers' poetry to her, the vitality of her soul's essence returned. She was so moved by the incisiveness of those profound perceptions, the rocks and boulders of those noble words. She was revived, captivated by the art of both Raoul and Jeffers, by the protean essence of their beings.

Why must she be so endlessly the fool, tempted by sociabilities that were less than regenerative, she wondered. All seemed a loss for her; only the riches of the spirit-world, the poetic genius of a Jeffers, a Raoul, or a Hesse could inspire her.

In the days before, she'd had too many houseguests, and her wild solitude had been torn asunder, leaving her in dread and despair. She'd considered either an early death or the emotional plowing offered by a psychiatrist.

Now, after the reading of her favorite poets and her union with Raoul, she felt replenished, sublimely reconnected. Here in the aviary with the fountain's music, life again streamed through her. She no longer felt suffocated by the plans and scenarios projected upon her. Life in its innocence offered a first breath again. Ah, if it was so simple, why didn't she live every day like this one? Why did she allow herself to become an instrument of desire and distraction? How could she let hypocrisy, hatred, violence inhabit her? Could she rationalize her peculiar fate by musing that the only way she could comprehend life was to experience its ragged brutality, living the edges so she could understand that the bed of roses *and* the crown of thorns were both aspects of the universal forces?

It appeared that life's events flourished with contradiction. On the one hand, she had to learn to disengage for her emotional survival. On the other hand, it was primarily her passion that pulsed her paintings and writing that fueled her soul with color and vitality. Detachment seemed to erase passion, and vice versa. How could she understand the countless faces of the gods without the direct experience of violence and wonder? Yet, the thirst of existence drank her blood like a vulture, leaving her at those times drained and useless. And she knew she bred her own merciless birds of prey that fed on her insatiably, especially when she was the most weary and vulnerable.

At certain times in her life, she soared like the dancer of her dreams. But invariably, the cycles would change, revealing death's face. Many of her family and close friends had died, etching her soul with sorrow. Now she lived more richly, embodying a greater depth, able to mock life's ironies yet to revere each moment.

She continued to ride the seesaw of life's contradictions, doing what she could to make a difference but accepting her limitations. She knew, for example, that the ill lovebird in the aviary would probably die despite her efforts. Still, she chewed on some seeds before leaving and placed them near the dying bird.

Then Raoul arrived. "Apparently the light needs the dark for its very existence," said Lara as she shared her reflections with him.

2001

THE OPPOSITES AS ONE

Is this a cycle of new beginnings
or a recycling of the past?

Is this rebirth and renewal
or deterioration and dying?

Is this a first bloom of love
or a final fade of flower?

The summer of my fruit
or the spoil of maturation?

The lie within the truth
or the truth within the lie?

Are not the opposites—one?

2000

BETWEEN WORLDS—BECOMING INVISIBLE

Entering columns of diaphanous mist, I pass through the visible membrane to become part of the invisible. Ah, to be unseen again, what a necessary relief. I re-found my exiled land, lost to me when I became entangled in the density of matter. It is easy to forget what you cannot see.

Immediately upon reuniting with my homeland, I found myself encircled by a white-winged dominion of angels. Flocked in their gossamer embrace, my own wings soon re-emerged. Spun by the angels' love, a luminescent cape of moonlight cast a halo over my crown, over the land.

In wonder, I again became the conduit of Mystery's unfolding, in my reverence for every plant and creature, in the offering of self to More. Here thrives the orgasmic essence, the elation of a union sublime. I had not sought this bounty with purpose. Rather, by extricating myself from the denser realms, I had become receptive and available. In the valuing of every ingredient of the alchemical process, the blessings, curses, and in-betweens, there spun a holy loom of internal regeneration, of integration. A glowing aura of awareness emanated as I breathed in the nurturing nights of the unseen, the ultimate luxurious intimacy of the invisible underlying the manifest—vintage grapes for the soul's wine.

Like a ghost with angels as silent companions, I drifted among ancestors, between transparent worlds where the living and the dead are one. I experienced the seething, brimming moment as pregnant with all that has been or ever will be, when the magic of synchronicities innocently confirms and mirrors existence.

I soared in this indivisible realm of transient freedoms, finding myself, to my surprise, soon engaged in dialogue with Monsieur Contradiction, a character visiting from the visible world. Strangely, yet appropriately, he was riding a black-and-white mule backwards through a desert of flaming rocks. Mirages (or were they my projections?) mirrored him on the dry desert plains—feigning spirit-water for thirsty wanderers.

I implored Monsieur Contradiction to reveal why, since life is composed of co-existing polarities, we are conditioned to believe that reality is either black or white. From the seesaw he now was riding, he replied, "When I am up I see things one way; when I am down, I see things another way. Yet I couldn't sit up without having sat down," he added with a chuckle, "so each is inherent within the other. Both the mellow day and the brutal storm co-exist. Observe these diversities with their ennobling tensions playing themselves out upon your heart-strings, upon the world's Aeolian harp." He paused as if to gather his breath.

I listened and then spontaneously responded, "I call it the unsame of the Same."[9] Then I moved invisibly while riding a musical note into the lyrical skies.

Before long, I spied below me a small, young girl seated under a dappled oak. This blond, curly-haired mistress called herself Princess Harmony. Sitting cross-legged on a log, she was gazing at a narrow stream trickling beneath her. Caped in the sun's gilded light, she chanted, "Ah, come and sit down beside me, so we can watch our reflections dancing as a duet in the stream. Let us gaze at the filigree of leaves silhouetting the sunset skies and listen to the birds' melodies."

Without hesitation I joined her, sitting on the shadow side of her sunny self. We were like chords in resonance; the stream mirrored our reflections in cadence.

Eventually, beckoned by a warm breeze of ascension, I departed and began to climb a steep, noble mountain slope flowering purple with burgeoning echium. I followed a narrow, winding path of white granite steps spiraling up to a forested peak high above the churning sea. While there, I encountered two rare poets who had woven their nests at Ranzibar, as they had named this colossal purple mountain surrounded by the sea's gardens, forests of towering sap-green cypress, and sentinels of nut-clad pine. I asked the first poet, who had the countenance of a bobcat, how he liked his mountain life.

He replied in a mellow, resonant tone, "My lament and longing are not eased by the ceaseless sea and its relentless breath of wind and fog. No, life for me is a battle without a war. I constantly struggle to redeem my suffering spirit from my body's chronic pain. Whether my battles are won or lost depends, it seems, on my courage." And as he uttered these mortal words, fed by his spirit's flames, the blood of his pen embroidered his poetic drawings upon an open page.

He continued to speak, confessing that death came regularly to his doorstep with long-fingered black gloves that clutched at his throat, suffocating his breath, grabbing his heart, constantly threatening his end. He elaborated, "Living amidst such splendor on this mountaintop offers the extremes of the elements and the challenges that are both internally and externally imposed and reflected."

I realized then that his exquisite poems and drawings were like the emblems of his spirit's battles, noble trophies born from his soul's journey, the music inspired by his continual triumphs over death.

Then Monsieur Contradiction drifted by like a vapor uttering, "But of course, can beauty be born without violence, without the abrasion for refinement?[10] What would Mistress Harmony say to that?" he mocked as he vanished into a fleeting, blue mist.

I wandered on, leaving this poet-bobcat in solitude at his rustic cabin. Then, just above his lair, I came upon the abode of another poet who had also spun her nest amidst the emerald gardens of Ranzibar. She had named herself Riva, guardian of the plants, flowers, and creatures.

She spoke of how she walked the poetic seams beneath the moon's gaze, ravished by the seamless space of this wilderness high, the tides' pulse chanting in cadence with her soul's rhythms. Listening to the breeze, seeing faces in the leaves, she was a servant to her soul's longings. Because she cherished her life as a psychic nomad, she knew that to travel in such ways required limiting her responses to the garrulous, purpose-filled world. She preferred the intimate, the impassioned, yet distanced sweep, the uncorrupted flow of the broad brushstroke. Sublime intuitions were her orienting antennae. Having known the exultation of distance-traveling, she grew bored and impatient with the anchoring distortions of the world's gravity. She regarded passports and security checks as the clutter and assault of the *manifest* world that has been mechanized by human modes of self-defense.

After the enchanted meeting with Princess Harmony, my reconciliation with Monsieur Contradiction, and my deep rapport with the male poet, I was ever more grateful for my explorative voyage to the invisible. In my blessed state I thanked and embraced the female poet-creature for her creative congeniality. And with sacred wonder, I realized I had found my twin soul-sister within, mirrored and at peace on the mountaintop.

2001

THIS OUTLANDISH SPECTACLE

A seething sea
roars black echoes
into the cave of my heart.

I thrive on the crest of wave,
the foam of churn.

Breathless, I yield to this wonder—
this outlandish spectacle called Life.

I walk the abyss,
an ennobling tension,
searching the horizon for balance
as the edge narrows.

And a subtle promise
of the Invisible World
still beckons.

2009

A STRANGE, GNARLY MAN

Today, I left home with the intention of taking a secluded walk, but ended up veering from my plan and visiting a strange, gnarly man who lived nearby in a cabin above the sea.

I thought myself to be irresistible, dressed in bright pink and red, but he closed the door before I could enter, explaining that he didn't feel well, that I should come back another time. Before the door was shut though, I caught a glimpse of his cave-like home filled with phantasmagoric figures carved out of stone—perhaps the stone of his heart. Although original, they were scary because they looked like weapons.

One stood tall and had a nose like a knife. Another was holding a heart behind a shield of metal. And still another was just a large mouth on long legs. They were inhuman creations; he and his statues were bloodless. I felt disturbed by his lack of hospitality and by his gallery of death, death of the heart. I mused that his inner life reflected the lack of humanity in the world, that today's survival was truly imperiled by this lack, since to be vulnerable is dangerous, especially in overcrowded, crime-ridden cities. Then I realized his inner cell resembled such a city, that this old gnarly man had woven his own ghetto, trapped himself in a self-spun web cast high above the sea.

Apparently the weapons his statues embodied were just what his heart had chiseled from life experience. But I couldn't help but wonder what had made his heart die, leaving him with the need for all those weapons. With the indifference of an inquisitive observer, I found him and his work to be most curious.

Who was I to make judgments about the myriad sculptures any of us may become in life, the molding of our clay? Yes, who was I, since I really don't believe in being a critic anyway. Opinions are subjective and should be thoroughly scrutinized. At least he is honest to his piss and vinegar—to the venom of his soul. One must question virtue. Many who claim to be virtuous merely use kindness as a subterfuge to obtain what they want.

Later that night, I dreamt that I fell into one of this strange man's sticky webs. When I did, he approached me with a glowing chest and radiant heart. He held me in his arms, which had suddenly become handsome and tawny. I somehow succumbed to his erotic seduction and allowed him to embrace me.

When I awoke, I thought how strange—the way he seemed in a waking state and then how he felt in the dream. Why bother to wake up to either reality? Certainly both realities are of each other. Why focus on just one? Indeed, a living paradox exists within this strange, gnarly man, as within us all.

2007

Lady Almond Blossom in Her Youth

IZABELLA AND AUGUSTUS

Izabella dwelled on a mountaintop. She was surrounded by wildlife—deer, bobcats, foxes, raccoons. Even lions could be seen prowling about. Seagulls, pelicans, cormorants, and condors hunted and bathed along the shores and beach cliffs below her refuge. Hummingbirds, blue jays, quail, and countless migrating birds came to her oasis to drink from the lotus fountain, to be shielded from the noise and pollution of that other world.

Next door, her pet-muse, Augustus, played his guitar into the coal-black night, composing rhymes and singing in verse. The breath of his spirit infused and animated the otherworldly rhythms he created.

Despite the autonomy of their individual lives, a silent synchronicity spoke of the spontaneous rhythms of their unified existence; this silent music between them was a timeless symphony of their destinies. Just as Augustus's melodies resounded with the pulse of the ocean's tides below, so their often unspoken language became a mirror of their secret souls.

Izabella and Augustus were fragile creatures, yet in their vulnerability thrived a courageous strength, a dedication to expressing their true essence through art. The countless dimensions of the game of life continuously revealed the unseen forces, the underlying dynamics, the innate contradictions.

Cora, a young girl born of tender passion, and Lady Almond Blossom, an aged sage, also lived with Izabella and Augustus. Cora grew vibrantly like a young filly in their gardens above the sea. Tenderly caring for a herd of white goats was one of her great passions. Sometimes she and the goats would kick up their heels and dance as Augustus serenaded them beneath the star-laden heavens. Although Cora attended a school nearby, she blossomed far more in her unique, untrammeled home life. On the mountaintop she learned about the care and health of plants, flowers, and trees, how to prune and nurture them. Cora was in dialogue with the elements, dancing at the twilight sunset, playing her flute and composing her own songs, expressing the part of her that extended beyond time and space. She and Augustus sang their souls as chords together, while Izabella, Lady Almond Blossom, the goats, and the birds swayed to their melodies.

Yes, this school on the mountaintop was far preferred to the world's systems of competition, ambition, and aggression. Cora's heart and soul were inspired by the Book of Life, the quality of precious, unhurried moments. She also had a passion for Lady Almond Blossom, who was now over ninety years old and spoke only occasionally. Her face wore the burnished hue of sunset, while her eyes, like blue blossoming stars, brightly glistened of infinity.

Through living example rather than spoken word, Lady Almond Blossom expressed her profound philosophy, her deepening wisdom and reverence for all of life's forces. She fully accepted, even revered, the dance of polarities, the flux of ever-changing tides, the necessity of refinement through abrasion.[11] Lady Almond Blossom knew the essentiality of detaching from life's overflow, of rejuvenating in the caves of night's secret kingdom.

Understanding that the innumerable masks of the invisible were to be seen-through as forces of the cosmic substance, she wasn't interested in responding merely to face values. Augustus, Izabella, and Cora embraced and honored this radiant being as the star of their future selves. In their varying cycles, as wildflowers in their seasons, they were all devoted to experiencing the uncorrupted moment. Pulsating with the tides, they were unique stars in orbit, in resonance on Earth.

When Izabella had driven into a nearby town with Augustus, she felt like a deer without horns amidst the mechanical cacophony of the traffic. In contrast, the temple-like school on the mountaintop was of an entirely opposite order. All of the Book of Life was a challenge and medium. They were like avatars sifting through layers of alchemical ingredients, unconsciously drawn to whatever life experience catalyzed further sculpturing of their being.

There was little lacking in the quality of their rich inner weavings. The gems of experience were in the acuity of their senses, passions, sensibilities, vulnerabilities. Yet when the precious strings of their instruments were played by the coarse world, these poets, free-falling into the moment, could succumb to a kind of corruption and want what others desired. They then became wingless, even more pathetic than domesticated humans. They could lose their artistic delicacy, the sensitivity that can only fully breathe from the Beyond. Only from that rare, poetic atmosphere could their wingéd art emerge.

Of course Izabella and Augustus knew they couldn't live in the timeless every moment, but austere urges ever beckoned in that direction. Like gray, wispy servants of a higher calling, these instinctive requests continually ushered them into that deeper, quieter, primal order where their roots could reconnect, restore, and be ever born into fresh beginnings.

One sunset, when Lady Almond Blossom was luxuriating in the last glowing beams of the sun's warmth, she gestured rather ceremoniously to the others to join her. She wanted them to know of a dream that had breathed her the night before. In her dream, their mountaintop revealed itself in splendorous colors. A boundless vortex of healing energies endlessly rooted and branched out, invisibly regenerating the surrounding energy fields with their radiance.

She encouraged Izabella and Augustus to continue to follow their sublime intuition, the songs of their souls. She also reminded them of the cosmic forces underlying the visible manifestations, behind the Earth's bizarre pageantry of parading puppets. Although wary of using words, she conversed with Cora about life's contradictions, how they were essential in the renewal of life, how the mountaintop was her soul's nest, her nexus of strength.

In order to maintain the fundamentals of their sacred school, she recommended that Cora continue to study, observe, and mix freely in the world of noise and opinion. Both the light and dark forces in their contrasting existence gave each other form and meaning. With this more expansive education, Cora could bring the sacred teachings from the mountaintop to others and be an essential messenger between worlds.

To these high-mountain dwellers, who called themselves psychic nomads, life was an adventure of discovery and wonder, and they used themselves as instruments in the exploration. In their reverence for every pulsing leaf, they resembled the ancient Chinese. In their need to dialogue with the rudimentary elements, to express their passion, to orchestrate the music of their souls, they attuned themselves to the seas and tides below, breathing in cadence with the Mystery. As barometers of the Earth's consciousness,[12] they were fulfilling sacred and challenging missions.

At times, it was demanding to be in this synchronicity, especially when the world was bringing the opposite so forcefully. But for this reason it became all the more essential to recognize the invisible world playing out the cosmic forces through them. Of course this defining was only a rope by which to pull themselves up when they had fallen and perhaps forgotten. Most of the time they lived in resonance with a metabolism of silent math in the ineffable symphony of the primal order.

They came to know both the tyrannizing winds of winter and the caressing breezes of summer as the unsame of the Same.[13] And they experienced these wildly polarizing forces internally as well—as ingredients of their very breath.

Meanwhile, the sun had descended and the air felt cool for July. These pan-human creatures felt the unity of their commonality and respectfully acknowledged their differences. In their rooted connectedness and regard, a tenderness sprouted that could change the world—even if subtly, if only within themselves.

2002

MOON HUNGER

The moon's white hunger
consumes me as I swim
beneath her iridescent gaze.

I become one with her,
with the light of sovereignty,
part of the shadows,
part of the beams.

My blood changes.
I transform into
another current of being,
a silvery naiad,
infused by the white hunger
of a symbiotic moon.

2011

THE BARON

for Edgar Allan Poe

In early summer long ago, on a moonless midnight, the Baron Ivan von Eickenstein arose after a dust-ridden sleep, as if lured out of his warm, blue chambers by night's starry realm. A path of gleaming white stones led directly from his lower balcony to a bluff above the sea, where a black lagoon, a pool of liquid nullity, awaited his full immersion.

With that first step into the hypnotic waters, he always experienced an enveloping release from the gravity of his being. The womb-like waters surrounding him became the elixir that could sew the seams of his torn soul and soothe his ragged, benumbed senses. Here, in these sacred waters, he could feel unnoticed, safe, half-wild again, like an innocent child. Perhaps, at last, the Baron could integrate his scattered selves, let them rise to the surface and become one with the rhythmic tides below. Here, with the sea as his only companion, perhaps the Baron could re-discover himself, resolve the mysteries of his inner violence and treachery—be healed.

In just the past few months, lost in a kind of delirium, he had murdered his closest consort, two officers in his army, and a few unnamed opponents. Thus, there was cause for his soul to be tortured. Even so, he lacked the awareness to comprehend fully the impact of his mad, savage behavior.

You see, the Baron did not live in a one-dimensional, black-or-white reality; he lived in many parallel worlds simultaneously. He moved all at once through the membranes of life's realities, its so-called truths and lies, as if he were peering through a kaleidoscope of illusions. How could his split self grasp the reality of his violent and macabre ways, the murder of those he professed to love?

Here, in the listless, fog-anchored night, he floated alone, seeking salvation, answers to his despair, his irreconcilable differences, the ongoing agonies between his angels and demons, his visceral war.

And how do we, dear Reader, dwelling in our own wars of polarities, find reconciliation?

How was he to make sense of those bones under the struts of his sumptuous bedchamber? Indeed, who could guess, upon entering his castle, that bodies lay rotting under the wine cellar? All appeared orderly, even fashionably elegant—the Byzantine carpet of dark blue velvet and gold, the marquis-shaped crystal beads of the chandelier, and the Austrian cut-glass decanter with one glass beside his lofty bedposts. No, it was quite impossible for anyone to conclude that behind the angular, quite handsome countenance of the Baron dwelled both a killer and a thief.

For countless generations, the men in his bloodline had been warmongers. Like his father before him, the Baron had pillaged every town he had seized, oppressing, plundering the townspeople, slaying anyone who challenged his power. By horrifying the townspeople in this way, he could take greater advantage of them. Fear, he recognized, was a cheap and ever-powerful weapon, and he and his army of merciless predators thrived on their power to oppress and destroy.

Ironically, the Baron often established himself as an ally of the local authorities. At least half the time, he and his army would feign devotion to the very people they later also plundered. Food, donations of money to the unfortunate, concern for the sick—all served as the Baron's camouflage. Yet, the strangest part of this story is that such a callous murderer would direct virtually all of his stolen wealth toward these kinds of altruistic endeavors. Apparently, in this way, he hid his tyrannical side not only from others but also from himself.

On this night, however, as the warm waters dissolved the locked dungeon of his soul, a poet-troubadour happened to wander up to the shores of the lagoon, strumming his guitar and singing of ancient worlds. He offered a richness of spirit the Baron had never before experienced. And here, after midnight in the gloom of heavy fog, the poet's lyrics, like the sea's concert below, entered the Baron's sick blood. The music re-metabolized the streams of his soul in a way that words alone never could. This unknown poet, this rhapsodist, had somehow mysteriously woven together the contradictory forces within the Baron. It was as if Ivan von Eickenstein had suddenly awakened from the death of his life and his soul had taken its first breath. Having absorbed the sacred music as if by osmosis, he felt magically transformed. And the reconciliation of his dualities carried him inwards, into the balm of newfound integration and bliss. The Baron had traveled far without moving, without his army, his servants, or his latest courtesan.

He took the hand of the young mystic, pleading with him to remain at his castle.

The tawny-mustached musician danced into a bow before so generous an offer, and promptly replied, "I cannot inhabit your luxurious palace, but I will meet you at midnight for as long as you wish, here in the silent noon of night, with the black wings of the Mystery to carry us. I will join you here by the shores of the sea's pulse, and dance and sing for you the forgotten language. But please understand," said the young man, "to pass through God's sacred gates, you must listen obediently to your soul, abandon your avarice and murderous instincts, and devote yourself to meditation as a way of life."

Ecstatic, trembling in his newfound state of grace and peace, placenta still wet behind his ears, the Baron gulped and replied passionately, without hesitation: "Yes, yes, of course. Is there anything else you ask of me?"

The minstrel responded in a mesmerizing tone: "Yes, send your collaborators away immediately. Live alone with your silence-starved soul until you become one with the symphony of creation. Only then will you grow the wings you need to rise above your demons. With your instincts wedded to higher intention, your behavior will no longer cause harm. Your soul will then be retrieved, and your suffering will cease. By purifying your heart in this way, you will manifest the divine."

2003

FROM VOID TO FLAME

As he swam
the remote, black lake of night,
he felt the ache of isolation.

Was he the last human still alive?
Was he close to anyone, anything?

Or had his heart
sunk to such despair
that he was numb?

Only anguish tinted
his void of nothingness.

Yet despite this overwhelming
black cell of despair,
the eternal night still glittered.

As he swam,
he let his many selves dissolve
into the soft, yielding waters
holding change
like undeveloped film.

His soul, immersed,
drank from these primal wells
alongside silent, sentient trees.

The void is the cocoon,
the womb of death's new flame
birthing a red tomorrow.

2004

ARTISTS' LOVE

As she greedily ate the spicy potato chips, she thought about how just moments ago she had been in the arms of her exotic lover. But they both accepted their intolerance for too much intimacy. And tonight, she knew that even as the fragrant breeze embraced the leaves, and planets beckoned from far distant lights, they must widow themselves again, drop the chain of their passion momentarily, and return to their solitary ways.

She continued to relish the spiciness of the chips as part of her withdrawal from him. The sensuous, silk canopy draping their bed looked forlorn. And the candle flames hungrily seemed to search the homeless air, while her world grew silent and dark as the vacant chambers of her soul.

How totally strange was this kind of love, a mysterious meeting of opposite chemistries, ebbing, flowing with a shoreline of its own. And yes, her lover was as mysterious and unknowable as the sea. "How grateful I am," she thought, not ever being able to explain their tidal rhythms.

He'd been gone for only twenty-five minutes, yet worlds had revolved since then. Her home seemed to expand in its emptiness. Like the despairing candle flames in the bedroom, her skin still glowed and ached for him. All her artwork on the walls seemed to cry out for appreciation. She had lost their perfect world and dissolved into the abyss, a deep-sea diver in the darkly brooding sea of the unconscious.

Having eaten too many spicy chips, her belly now hurt. Wasn't love like that? And passion, too, for that matter? Her stomach felt ready to burst, just as their perfect world had exploded.

She should have been more conscious about what she consumed, since her body was already hurt. Yesterday, she had inadvertently injured a rib at the pool in an effort to turn a ladybug back on its feet. Now it was difficult to move. And to injure oneself trying to save an insect—how ludicrous! Why wasn't she in her body enough to be more careful? What a perfect fool she was!

And now, after being greedily excited by her lover and then greedily devouring too much of another kind of spice, she dragged herself into the living room and sought relief in a reclining chair. The wind was screaming crazily outside. Should she ask her lover to return and offer solace? Or do herself in with more spicy chips? Perhaps a bath with Epsom salts would help, she thought, her once perfect dream now churning in her belly.

Why did they always go to such extremes, she wondered. They seemed the antithesis of each other, yet they connected deeply through their art, music, and unspoken rhythms, which collided, fused, and were ever in concert. Yes, the creative process mysteriously manifested through them.

Earlier in the day, she had been mesmerized by the echoing breakers below and the sight of the seagulls drifting like white popcorn on the coppery kelp beds. And later that afternoon, the heat wave of their passion had been reborn, a surprise to both of them. Spontaneously they were resonating and blazing together again.

Even though he had been gone for forty-five minutes now, her flesh was still glowing with unrequited desire. She consoled herself with the thought that a bath would soon soothe love's ailments. As she submerged herself in the tub, she felt like a nurse caring for an ailing patient. Meanwhile, the house had settled down amidst the dark curtains of night.

Not only did these artists live on the rocky cliffs above the sea, they also lived their raw edges as a way of life. They repeatedly took the media of themselves to the precipice. Often, they became so alienated and isolated in their wanderings and searches that when back together, filled with their own gold, they barely recognized each other. Their enigmatic attraction was continually surprising to both of them.

And tonight, after bringing their gems together, fusing their fires, they again would have to die along with their embers, as widowed beings, lovers who must forever give themselves up to the beginnings, even though it was only a possibility that the endings would result in new inventions, as creation is ever unknowable. And often their moments of ecstasy were unmercifully cast into the abyss like sacrificed pagans. What a strange way to live and to die. What an odd yet enchanted life, to be cliff-dwelling chameleons.

Now, an hour since his departure, the haunt still persisted, but her stomach began to feel better. From the tub, she reached for the phone and made an appointment for the next day. It was painful, letting the warm fragrance become diluted so quickly. But what other way was there to let go?

The warm Epsom salts seemed to mock yet console her primitive animal self as she soaked in the tepid hospitality. All the precious pollen of their passion went down the drain in the indifferent water. "And so it is," she scoffed.

Then she called her lover to let him know how insufferable their separation had been for her. "Yes, we're like cannibals," he exclaimed when she told him about the potato chip orgy. She retorted with a laugh, "If there were a pizza parlor nearby, you'd probably have binged too." He agreed in a rather depleted tone and added that, after their ultimate passion, he also had become lost and disoriented and had sunk into feeling like a deplorable beast.

"Our luminous worlds, abundant with erotic pomegranates, have burst their delicate skins, leaving brave memories to shiver in the Void. These naked feelings are now orphans in an indifferent house slumbering on a lone cliff," she wrote in her journal, and then fell into the welcomed relief of sleep.

2007

FREEDOM'S TIDES

The thrashing, biting wind
shakes my soul,
but the fertile essence
of your music feeds me.

The ripping cold
shrinks my heart,
but my passion
for your lyrics beats on.

The groove of fear
threatens imprisonment,
but the vistas of your rhythms
have no boundaries—
and freedom's tides carry me.

The thorns of humanity's crown
prick my pale flesh,
but your creative rivers
fill my ragged ravines with song.

Heavy skies oppress my soul,
erasing my dreams,
yet I snuggle between
the god of sensuality
and the god of spirituality.

Luxuriating in this embodiment,
I let the birds carry me
on freedom's tides—
wingéd white in the sun.

2008

A LOVE AFFAIR OF THE POLARITIES

They had been lovers for nearly twenty years now. Jade, a first generation Chinese-American, who was an herbalist, had enormous, tragic eyes and displayed grief in every gesture, as if her heart had been broken and everything about her life was futile. Her delicate, emaciated frame appeared eaten away by something or someone. Her lover, Anatole, a psychologist, was a lusty, olive-skinned man of Siberian descent with an almost affectionate violence about him. Despite his fevered energy, his voice emanated melancholy.

Over the years, the lamenting Jade and the not less pitiful Anatole had gradually descended into mere phantoms of their former selves. They were in the winter now of what once had been a most fruitful union, where love was lived in innocent magnanimity. These days Jade was obsessed, muttering continuously about what she felt Anatole or the gods had stolen from her. She limped along, her life severed from the wells of spirit, torn from another time when life was simpler and more joyous, when human beings were different, before the stem of the world-core had rotted. She had allowed the ashes of their struggle to accumulate in a deep grave of sorrow, walking around as if she were a coffin, her heart marked by a blood-drenched cross.

And Anatole strode about continually restless, somewhat disembodied, anxiously trying intellectually to make sense of it all, speaking in a controlled monotone, although his temperament was incendiary. A psychiatrist of brilliant discernment to his numerous clients, he was somehow unable to recognize the severity of his mate's malaise. And even if he had, he could not have acted differently.

Having both been seduced by the darker realms, Jade and Anatole had lost their discernment. Their essence had become skeletal and crumbled like dry bones at their feet. The two spent most of their time fueled by an irreconcilable turmoil within, a longing to uncover their souls' path, although the way to this discovery was not clear. An obsessive kind of self-absorption prevailed, burdening the atmosphere around them. What was this lovers' illness that possessed them with suffering and violence? Were Jade and Anatole merely marionettes of the Cosmic Whim, compelled by archetypal forces, with their shadow-sides temporarily running the show?

They showed up at their respective jobs and social functions, presenting sane and dutiful fronts. But when they weren't engaged in the obligatory, mundane activities of their daily lives, they were embroiled in personal conflicts, in some form of lusty love madness turned violent.

Were physiological imbalances contributing to this turmoil? Or did they need to taste each other's blood to feel truly alive? Did they need to die to each other continually to be reborn? And how different is love from death or the battlefields of war? Are we witnessing through Jade and Anatole the acceleration of random instincts typical of those we might witness during catastrophic cycles? If the caveman's instinct pulses our very blood and routine instincts can run us like rats in a maze, is there really such a thing as civilized? Don't masks of civility merely conceal the beast within?

Perhaps instincts in varying degrees always run the show. And decorative smiles and elaborate costumes are required uniforms of acceptable behavior, merely dressing up the instincts that are the root of all our behaviors. Are Jade and Anatole merely cosmic puppets, conduits of the indifferent forces? Aren't we simply the forces of history dressed up? [14]

Perhaps the magical and popular word "love" is really a subterfuge, a subliminal word that represents the biochemistry of entangled polarities. Like our immune systems with their red and white blood cells, apparently love too has its armies of opposites—shadow dancing unconsciously. Why should passion as a pro-life force not include its opposite? In this case, Jade and Anatole might murder each other on their personal battlefields, having once enjoyed the nectar of tender rapport. Clearly corruptive forces invaded their once-fertile union, as can so easily happen. Base instincts and tenacious weeds of past conditioning overran the ephemeral ground of their earlier passion, suffocating their ideals. But militant and automatic modes are an organic part of the jungle's procreation, spawning the Miracle in all its atrocities and splendor.

Yet is love any different now than it was in ancient times when primitive rituality and sacrifice prevailed? Perhaps it's not love that has changed but simply the styles of its expression. And apparently we are still, at heart, the same savages, only in these times wearing more sophisticated gear, roaming the world, shedding blood as a way of living. If that is the case, perhaps we may find solace in the words of Nikos Kazantzakis, "The greater the bloodbath, the greater the rebirth."

An untold history is being revealed as the human mutates in acceleration, transforming amid the grist of the technological revolution. Yet, in these catastrophic times, we must question if it is possible that the human species never really evolves, that the pendulum merely swings back and forth, that we are both propelled and limited by our survival instincts.

Perhaps what the world soul thirsts for is an archaic revival[15] of the ancient traditions based on comprehension of the powers of nature and the wisdom of the masters. Perhaps we could, for example, re-enliven the energy fields of the Minoan days, the Greek mythologies that embrace the goddesses and gods within each of us, celebrating the fresh breath of life's origins. How different life would be for us, the Jades and Anatoles of this world, if our hearts blossomed from the insights born of our previous ignorance and struggle, if we could liberate our spirits and reconnect our souls to our rightful heritage.

2005

A MEMORY LIKE THE SUN'S

A memory like the sun's
forgets the storm.

Without accumulation,
does time exist?

Yet, we are here
in this ephemeral whisper
that could, for an instant,
murmur of freedom—
that elusive eternity
that pleads for expansion,
a moment's reprieve
in the waking timeless.

Here, we can escape
the plight of being human—
and fling our mortality
like dirty laundry,
beyond lament,
into the hungry sea.

2006

HAUNT OF THE DARK TWIN

Part of her was tortured by despair, as if the world had nothing more to offer. She felt either indifferent towards or bored by what others enjoyed. Their talk seemed insubstantial. After years of naïveté, she now saw through the illusions.

At times, she felt fulfilled by her study and artwork, her psyche's explorations and evolving perceptions, but tonight, after a productive day, the haunting returned. What would silence this plaintive cry? The passion of a new romance? A more intimate rapport with her lover? Out of the gap came a scream for something, for someone.

She'd been blessed with everything one could desire: health, creativity, beauty, intelligence, lovers, friends, wealth, travel. But of course, along with these gifts came challenges. Although she still felt youthful and attractive, she was haunted by the realization of an encroaching mortality. And then there were the tasks and dependencies required by the maintenance of everyday life—leaving her lost to weariness and longing for the nurturing of her soul's essence.

This haunt was like a dark twin who could re-appear without warning, at times when she least expected it. When this shadow inhabited her, she felt estranged from herself, the world, her intimate companions. Perhaps she was anxious that she might be stuck in the bottleneck of this emergence, that this transition might be just a treadmill going nowhere, that she'd already experienced the benevolence of life's glories and all that remained now was gradual deterioration and death. She didn't want to believe this, but it was possible, regardless of whatever else fate held for her.

Perhaps she'd been isolated for too long from everyday life, yet somehow she never felt secluded enough. Solitude brought some of her most sacred and exultant moments.

Tonight the opposites, doubt and faith, orchestrated her reality and the dark twin ruled.

At least she could write about it. That was the exorcism, the elixir to expunge the phantom lament.

2002

THE DIAMOND BUCKLE
for Leonard Cohen

She was partly turned on
and partly turned off.
And in between
was her diamond buckle
sewn onto an old leather belt.

Yes, partly turned off
and partly turned on—
passionate in dream,
a discomfort with life.

Yes, on and off
with a diamond buckle
and the old leather belt,
demanding she live.

Then blossomed a springtime
when her rhythms swept her
beyond her belt—
and threw away the buckle.

She ran free as a child
dancing with the wind.
And the wild beasts
devoured her discomfort.

Life had digested her anew
and by some mysterious token
lent beat to her once-withered heart.

She rode on the back
of a white egret's tail
and dropped her fallen self
to the sea—
watching it dissolve into salt.

2006

CHAPTER 5

GRIST FOR THE SPIRITUAL MILL

Horse in Anguish

TODAY'S BARBARIANS

Today's barbarians
have bulldozed the road,
leaving it level and clear.
Yet the way ahead
is riddled with puzzles.

And the dust has obscured our illusions—
we pant up invisible stairs
to a tower of vanishing dreams.

Up the valleys, down the dales,
the red whispers pursue us
and the demons taunt.

Gradually the shadows
that accompany us
on our leonine hunt
fade in the sun's insistence.

Yes, today's barbarians lead the way,
a journey not for the faint of heart.
And like fools, we follow.

2009

FEARITA

Once there lived a tiny creature named Fearita who had been running and running ever since she was a young child. All this running had made her so small that she couldn't be seen, not even with a microscope. From what was she running? This terrorized, almost invisible creature was trying to escape from a monster with an enormous mouth. The monster, named Señor Past, constantly attempted to seduce Fearita with glittering illusions about days gone by.

The Señor continually robbed Fearita of her potential by hiding on dark days, then suddenly leaping from the shadows to dust her with a sprinkle of Past. Immediately, Fearita would be infatuated by what once glittered, and then the monster would inhale her. Afterwards, he would dump her fragmented being onto an alien patch of land, and she would be digested by her memories. Disoriented, Fearita would then become even more fearful, unable to live in the present moment.

Because it isn't possible to see the past clearly with present eyes, Fearita just kept running, hoping she could outrun this monster. But this strategy never worked; there was such an accumulation of worn-out programs.

Then at last, this tiniest creature in the world realized that if she allowed herself to be repeatedly consumed by Señor Past, she would finally be too small ever to re-enter the present. This realization illumined every atom of her being, enlivening her courage, liberating her spirit. And she began to evolve with increasing presence into the moment.

This creature with wildflower eyes and ever-changing colors now embraces a multi-dimensional view and purrs with possibility. Renaming herself Valorina, she thrives, a universal creature fearless enough to live freely in the now.

And although her visible self is now similar to that of other creatures, her invisible spirit breathes of the boundless.

1984

BARE ESCAPE

Drowned by memory,
I drag myself
up from the galloping sea,
only to sink again into
the quicksand of illusion.

I summon every fiber
of strength to duel
with a past seduction
as I dodge
the next thundering wave.

A bolt of insight illumines.
Yesterday's realities dissolve,
and I breathlessly gasp,
inhaling the fresh oxygen
of a bare escape.

2004

INTRO-VICTOR, CREATURE OF MANY POCKETS

Intro-Victor considered himself to be utterly unique. He had a slim, white, pliable body with many limbs of varying lengths and colors. His arms, legs, and hands moved constantly inward toward the countless leather-like pockets he had woven from his desires, plans, and ambitions. Sometimes it was hard to distinguish his hands from his pockets, as they were constantly enmeshed. Often he was so tied up with his many grasping hands and the enclosing grip of his many arms around his body that he looked as if he were going to implode, strangled by his own tendrils.

He would have preferred to force his numerous limbs into some favorite activity, one that filled him with pleasure. But he was so trapped within himself that he could only respond robotically to his pockets and their demanding appetites.

Strolling around Lake Como in the Italian Alps near the alpine lodge where he resided was the only pastime that seemed to relax his muscles. After walking for hours, he would lie down under a tree and feel what it was like to be vibrantly alive. Miles and miles of filigree-fine muscles in his arms and legs would start to unwind and extend over great distances. Then he could touch, smell, see, and feel the joy of everything throughout every cell of his being. From this relaxed state, he beheld the world around him, the peaks, the lake, with new eyes. He lost interest in his pockets. His hands no longer grasped. He was as loose and free as a Taoist.

When he was in this Zen flow, he could choose to do wondrous things. Perhaps he would roll up all his limbs in harmony, take a dip in the cobalt blue waters, and later imbibe a little moon-luster on his cheeks. Why not play for a while, he mused dreamily, gazing into the green eyes of an exotic dragonfly that had landed on his knee.

He is not as strange and unusual as he thinks. If he spoke to others of his entanglements and his pockets, he'd find he had countless kin.

1987

EXTRA-VERA

Extra-Vera was the exact opposite of her brother Intro-Victor. Physically she had the same slim, white, pliable body with many limbs of myriad sizes and colors. But whereas Intro-Victor's moved inward, her arms and legs moved constantly outward into the material world.

Extra-Vera was constantly whirling, sometimes in circles, sometimes forward, other times in reverse, as if wildly blown about by a tornado. She was really only satisfied when she moved in a forward direction. Being in constant motion and having limbs that spontaneously flung out, she obviously could not control her direction and would often find herself caught in boring, retro activities.

She was not entrapped like Intro-Victor with his inside pockets, but rather with outward pockets into which she had spun a value or desire. Perhaps these exterior pockets were necessary to satisfy her hands, grasping arms, and flinging legs. Like Intro-Victor, Extra-Vera also wanted to scream when she felt her grasping limbs were running her life. Then after a cycle of this wildly extraverted, perhaps unchosen activity, she too needed just to hang loose for a while. Her limbs could then rest and respond only to her more discriminating urges, rather than to so many leather-like pockets asking to be spun or satisfied.

When she dropped into this hang-loose rhythm, Extra-Vera felt as ecstatic as Intro-Victor. Her arms, legs, and hands would then uncoil and spread out as an intricate metropolis, appearing like Los Angeles from a jet. And when she was not being carried by the energy of grasping, her favorite moments happened effortlessly, in rhythms of playful experimentation. In this Zen-like stance, she was her most creative.

1987

SNIPPETS OF OURSELVES

I couldn't help but notice that he was projecting on me throughout our conversation. He had his psychological shears out, pruning and snipping what I would say and making my expressions his own. I knew he was under great duress and needed these cuttings for his own barren garden. He needed my seeds to fertilize his own, to grow flowers—even if they were germinations stolen from me. I knew he would only use what he could integrate, so it didn't really feel like theft.

Perhaps that is something of what friendship offers—snippets of ourselves that those identifying with us can attempt to replant and cultivate in their own gardens. Each of us, in our own style, does the same.

2008

A STRANGER IN SAN FRANCISCO

As he wandered outside the café, away from the crowd, to have a smoke, a tall, forlorn woman approached him, as if out of nowhere. She told him he was attractive and then asked some casual questions in a somehow comforting way: "Where do you live? Are you enjoying the evening?"

Strangely, this odd, starving creature seemed fully to see him, more than his lover with whom he was traveling. When she asked for some coins, it was with a kind of hurried pleasure that he searched his pocket for a twenty-dollar bill. And with relieved excitement, he handed her the money, most grateful for this strange and unexpected break in his isolation.

2007
outside the Café International

ASSAULT ON THE SENSES

When I returned home from the city, scenes of relentlessly glaring computers, headlights, and the hyper-mechanics of civilization still flashed through my being. Having absorbed that static, I continued to carry it within.

Tonight, the ceaseless overcharge of the city still obliterates my inner wilderness, crushing my seed, obscuring the inscrutable heavens above and the dreaming mountains beyond. Silence has been corrupted, the fruit of evening's blackness invaded by the lingering assault on my senses.

Like me, the stars seem disoriented, alien, glittering with a surreal light, stumbling and lost upon the slumbering mountains.

2001

A PREMATURE LAMENT

Like a tigress lying in wait, I listen for the sound of your footsteps at my bedroom door. I hear only the uncaring pulse of the tides below. How foolish I am, I weep, to have let you go. How could this happen? It seems unfair. I pray to the Mystery, to trust the Tao with its indifferent plow to rake us back into the now. Let us bow, stepping out of each other's way.

I step out of my own way and listen again for your footsteps. Will they return? Knowing what once was is now dead, I lie in wait, hoping our ghosts will orchestrate a new dance. The past has drowned, dropping away like lead.

Listening instead to the echoing sea, I give up the memory of your approaching footsteps. Relieved, I crawl inside the opening moment. The night soothes my rawness, quiets my sorrow. Letting the pulse breathe me, I yield to the moment.

With reverence for the Mystery that brought us together and now flings us apart, I sing with the currents that wash our footprints away. Our rhythms continue to ebb and flow as the melodic tides below. Let us not mourn what we still have.

2003

ONE WINTER NIGHT

How does one survive
the grimness of winter,
when even the white rose
is too pale to emit any scent . . .
When the joy and pain of things
leaves one stranded
on biting shores . . .

When love has become too distant . . .
When even the sun
denies its own existence
and the opaque skies hide their stars
with a selfish grin?

Tears are too priestly
for the pathetic suffering
that bleeds through these raw words.

Yet to feel bereft
in the calm of night
reveals more than words ever can.

Silence alone speaks tonight.

And I yearn to listen,
sensing there is more.

2010

LONELINESS

Loneliness can enshroud the atmosphere with a chilling haunt, revealing a void within. This void, with its peculiar autonomy, can be felt in crowds as easily as when alone. Yet, during these times, by yielding to the soul's cries, we can open ourselves to possibilities of deeper reflection and understanding.

Why not acknowledge this loneliness when it appears, keep it company, releasing it to another host.

The experience of solitude *without* loneliness offers us a sublime and flowering state of self-containment, a sacred inner kingdom.

2009

DON'T GIVE BLOOD TO THE GHOSTS

Before he departed that afternoon, Gabriel, her exotic, dark bird of a man, had warned her, "Don't get involved with the ghosts." Those weren't his precise words, but that is what he meant.

That night, on Gabriel's return, the exchange between them had been intense; it felt as if they each had breathed their last breath of life and of passion into the other. Finally, they had agreed it was over. And he had said, "I'll get out of your way."

Lying on a divan across from him, Amanda felt she should have been relieved. After all, she had been driving him away for months. But instead, she found herself staring at her feet—thinking how small they looked, how small she was. There was nowhere she wanted to go, nothing she wanted to do, no one else she wanted to see.

Amanda had succeeded in convincing Gabriel that they were emotionally incompatible, that he didn't *know* her—that he couldn't provide the solace, the intimacy she needed. But when she thought about losing her lover of four years, she felt hollow. Her redwood home, its high beams and spacious shadows lit by pulsing candlelight, seemed to shudder in loneliness. Suddenly it felt vacuous and sterile. Amanda wept, distraught, in the desert of her inner chambers. Gabriel slunk deeper into the divan facing her, listening to her assessment of everything that was wrong with him. Then he put his shiny, indigo-feathered wings around her, as if to shield her, perhaps from herself.

Storms had drenched their haven perched high upon the mountain cliffs on the Dragon's Crown. The angry sea below arose in threatening, overwhelming waves. As Amanda sobbed, she remembered a poem she had written for Gabriel before they lived together, a poem about how their lovemaking synchronized with the water-chimes of falling rain. And she cried even more, unable to feel his wings, his cloak of protection. She felt the grief of one who has just murdered her ideal self, one who has unconsciously destroyed all she cares about.

That night, Amanda reclined upon her rumpled bed, her auburn hair tousled. She struggled to interpret the meanings behind the challenges of these past few months. Why had this happened? Had she been possessed by ghosts of the past? It all seemed to occur without her knowledge, beyond her control. It was as if she had a screen in the back of her head, and others had invaded, projecting their movies in which she starred in roles she would never have chosen.

Then that evening, in a luminous streak, she had a vision. The reel of a different kind of movie sped through her mind, revealing the dynamics underlying life's myriad masks. Every insight, like a fractal of truth, contributed to the formation of a mosaic-mirror of multi-faceted revelation.

Amanda knew the accumulated conditioning of the past could carry the anchoring gravity of centuries, could make it difficult to change, to be open to new things. But when the past carries patterns so immobilizing that they suffocate the present or our ideals for the future, she knew that we must create new perceptions and behaviors. Otherwise we just serve the wailing ghosts of our ancestors who drink our blood without consent.

Amanda became aware that her situation was not simply the drama being acted out with Gabriel but was also a story about the ghosts who were playing out repetitious, discordant tunes on the piano of her mind.

Many years later, when Amanda had become more detached from the situation, she wrote, "Before these ghosts terrorize and de-harmonize the whole being, their masks must be torn off—their essence recognized. Living or dead, seducing or protesting, their truth must be revealed."

1987

O ILLUSIONS

O illusions that twirl around me, your shadows haunt me, mocking my serious brow. When, if ever, will I move like the tides upon the ancient sands, forgetting everything that has gone before—just being the ebb and flow. When will I be like the sun, without memory, just blazing and vanishing, not beholden to habit or routine.

O illusions that dance me, let me go to the light. Let me be as a prism, free from the human stage, fresh as the first face of dawn. Then I'll mock *you* and soar high, beyond your tease, no longer your puppet.

2010

IN SEARCH OF THE RED

A frozen castle stands,
awaiting winter's bitter thrust.
Its garden lies dormant,
pale with patience.

A rose bush weeps
that its roots are so deeply buried
it cannot run away.

And the trees bend and bow
in the howling wind,
yielding to their fate.

Somehow the birds
seem to have escaped
by the glory
of their feathered wings.

But you and I remain
separate and bound.
Our frozen havens
and the biting air
capture us without care.

The meadow of our love
cries out with emerald urgings,
When will we be able
to commune again?
And can we still hold hands
in the bleakness of unspoken feelings?

Or must I depart like a wild gypsy
to search elsewhere for the red of life?

2009
inspired by John Keats, as portrayed in the film Bright Star

RIVA'S JOURNAL
for Hermann Hesse

With her titian tresses illumined in the sun's beams, Riva sat in the aviary writing in her journal: "So-called realities are increasingly becoming meaningless. Dates, titles, awards, ambitions all seem ludicrous. The world appears to be run by mega monsters of corporate greed, vanity-based illusions, the poverty of insatiable appetites. Spawned by fear and defenses, these distortions lead to the destruction of what is authentic and would otherwise be free in life. How do we humans so easily waste what is most precious by trading the essential for the extraneous? This bizarre contagion has reached epidemic proportions. In this eleventh hour, it is time to re-examine priorities, re-define value systems, and experience a more enriching quality of life."

Riva's lover, Roberto, sat across from her, strumming chords on his guitar and harmonizing with the rippling currents of the sea below. Riva continued to write about her need to relinquish that which fettered her soul's sacred stirrings. Only the breath of the sacrosanct moved her, yet seemed ever more elusive.

It was time to breathe fully in the moment, to be in the timeless, outside of human measurements, stereotypes, and concepts. She yearned to reconnect with the Source, feel the wet soil under her weary feet, experience the tropical parrots with their flowering feathers, and watch them drink from the sparkling waters of the aviary fountain. How she loved to bathe the lovebirds with a light spray of water and observe them thrill as their wings bloomed, their eyes closed in ecstasy, as if they were little feathered Buddhas.

Riva noticed the tame parrot Solange becoming close to a female parrot named Laura.[16] In the mini-ecology of the aviary, Riva could study their courting habits, which were far more civilized and subtle than human dating games. With his beak roving dangerously close to her eyes, the male preened the fluorescent feathers of his mate. Her trust was the crown of gems that wedded them.

After all the human-created complexity, only the simple seemed to enchant Riva. Only the innocence of her soul's heart let her senses thrive in the sanctity of night's dark caves and bathed her in the sublime luxury of the eternal.

Recently, she had been forced into an arena of distortion by a relative whose greed knew no bounds. He had apparently adopted a strategy of self-righteousness to disguise his treachery and betrayal. He was a young beast trying to push an elder out of the herd so he could take over. Riva was forced to become defensive and aggressive in order to preserve her rights.

From this cyclone of toxic energy and the suffering that resulted, came a rebirth of what truly mattered to Riva—a rebirth of passion for the quality of life she had woven. She knew she must live in the grace of her Taoist urge, following her intuitions as the tides of the moon, listening to the lyrics of the chanting sea. She must not allow herself to be separated from the essence of the simple and ecstatic, from spiritual richness and passion for the deeper meanings that crowned her life's intention.

Meditating in the intimate dark caves of her inner world restored her dreams—her imagination blossomed. But the anxiety, dysfunction, and chaos of family politics and those of the world left her feeling alienated and disenchanted.

Nevertheless, she still beheld autumn, in the crisp yellow leaves drifting to earth, in the river's diminishing flow, in the haunt of the waning moon. She felt the wane in her own being and was curiously relieved. Words had become cumbersome and talk had become wearying. The voracious avarice erupting from the family had seared her heart with a strange blue fire, and yet the ashes of suffering now glimmered as embers of new insights. The invasion of these abrasive forces had reinforced her impulse to stay separate from the density of materialistic appetites and remain devoted to spiritual freedom as her singular path.

Challenges repeatedly presented their opposing forces. By affirming her values over those destructive scenarios, she had triumphed. But how often was Riva willing and able to lose blood to the predators? In the future, would she be able to screen out the toxins, observe which of her own behaviors fed the wrong appetites, and avoid some of these grisly encounters?

As she reclined in the aviary and listened to the fountain's lyrical waters, Riva watched tiny chipmunks share seeds with the multi-colored lovebirds and sun conures. Even with a reverence for the Tao, Riva realized one could get trapped in the fangs of the all-pervading predators. But now that the ordeal was over, she saw it as part of a greater regeneration and refinement, remembering the forces that breathe us also make fools of us, doing with us as they will.

Riva recognized that with awareness and sublime intuition to guide us, we can re-alchemize the cosmic ingredients we encounter. When we accept the mystery of the seeds allotted us, we can become the fruit of our trees, forever in wonder at life's essence and its myriad manifestations.

2002

THE SILENCE BREATHING

The sun is too hot
for our knowing.

When night falls,
a new freedom is released—
in the silence breathing,
in a jealousy emitted
by the cold, distant stars.

The moon, too indifferent
to care about the garden's thirst,
simply shines and moves on.

Our wretched human drive
is weary of itself—
only finding relief from
its crowded freeways when lost.

Dawn shrugs from a sense of duty
like a sleazy harlot, unrecognized.
With mystery and craftiness,
she takes the form of twilight,
reborn in the blue robes of Eve—
calm, collected, and impenetrable.

2011

RECLAIMING MY KINGDOM

I feel intense and expansive relief from reclaiming the temple of my soul.

I congratulate myself for rescuing my inner kingdom and releasing it from karmic ties, from ties that imprison. How different is the sanctity of my personal haven from that of other dominions or systems of government? If I allow disregard, I'm just adding to these imbalances in the world; I am feeding the brute, motivated by baser dynamics, who takes charge not because of any authentic claim. I am contributing to the kind of behavior exhibited by many world leaders who plow ahead on automatic, purely for self-interest, ignoring the rights of their citizens.

To act without regard for others infuses a toxicity that disorients and drains. Such predators hunt their prey with rabid instincts, fueling their power from behind what are often indiscernible masks. Whether these despots are motivated by ignorance or fanaticism, the true value of life escapes them. Trails of pollution and misdeeds, the crimes of the world, follow in their wake. This domination uses intimidation to undermine integrity.

How many of us are willing to see our plight? How can we as individuals exercise our rights and awareness, restore our dignity?

Can awareness alter our genetic programming? Or are the shoes we are cast made of stone?

Perhaps by re-discovering our soul's essence, we can unite with our spiritual kin, emerging with the consciousness necessary for a new future.

2006

FERAL WEATHER

The enigmatic climes of Big Sur offer an example of how to live our lives. Retaining no memory of the last storm, last sunset, last gust of wind, each instant is born anew. Isn't memory a most powerful jailer?

Feral weather expresses the gods, powers that govern beyond human conjecture. Like puppets, we are forced to yield again and again with humility to the Ultimate, which employs us with indifference.

2006

AS A FLAG

Over the years, pieces
of my selves have died.

The winds of time
have hurled themselves
relentlessly against my anthem.

I stand now as a flag
to my experiences—
tattered and worn,
on the cliff's edge,
gazing out to sea.

Yet I keep singing
like a bird
after the storm,
like the sun-drenched day—
smiling with innocence
after the wind's assault.

Falling again into
the eternal moment,
I bow like a wavering flag
before the sun.

2004

CHAPTER 6

QUINTESSENTIAL CREATORS

Pregnant with Creation

THE POET

In the aquamarine
of the ocean's blood,
in the covey of hunting birds
chasing the yellow tail
of lost sunset—
your essence thrives.

The gardens, bursting in flower,
bow to your poetic splendor,
but can they care beyond their petals?

Aren't you, the poet,
answering to a destiny
greater than yours alone?

In you, the irreconcilable forces
meet, battle, copulate—
and out of this bloodshed
poetic tapestries form,
intricacies of the terrible and the sweet,
of famished eagles
and black scorpions meeting
in the red night,
clashing in invisible darkness
where fragile birth
takes its first emerald breath.

Is that where you go,
O valiant and violent poet
of colliding worlds?

What brazen cave can hold
your flames without explosion?
What white arms can console you
without being torn?

What moon will betroth you,
halo your burning feet
and bear the glowing ash—
as you wed the only one
who doesn't melt
in the blaze of union.

2007

THE ARTIST'S CABIN

He stalks about his studio, breathing from invisible worlds. Poetic verses unfurl—rich, fertile carpets to the unknown, endless skins of him cast into endless paintings. Part lion, part velvety brown valley bear, he is nourished by the red nipples of merciless gods and goddesses who possess him. Their milky-scented jasmine swirls from his navel. His dancing flames fuse with mine in blazing revelry.

The emerald grasses chase after him, capturing his fertile moments as he springs. He exhales invisible red and black flowers that faint on paper, damning his cabin walls with revenge. With all the paintings, paintings, paintings tacked onto the mocking walls, his magical studio soars in chameleon rapture.

He leads the endangered species list as he walks the perilous edges of creation's abyss.

2009

THE MALE CANARY

A panhuman male had illuminated the land, lighting up dead souls and sorrow-filled hearts, adding an extra pulse to the rain's beat, extra warmth to the winter's blue cold. The naked trees with their bare arms blushed in his presence. It was as if he were reborn, but not into *another's* religion—into his own, as a soul-crying, guitar-playing poet. Rays of golden feelings poured from the myriad tongues of his spirit's voice, embracing the atmosphere. Like a raving male canary, he offered his essence through song. Like storm-fed rivers dancing to the seas, his poetry flowed from the caves and coves of a sacred yearning. It was as if, until now, he had been hibernating all his life, waiting for the first breath of spring to gush into his lyrics. As his poetry currented into musical forms, new shapes were continuously born into existence. Emotions merged with an ancient resonance; the haunt of unfamiliar worlds exploded into meters of color and image.

Lured by his wails into the vacant stare of moon, the Siren of the beach cove below, with her long, green seaweed hair, climbed the gossamer spiral of lament up to his lair above the sea. Here, with the full scarlet moon of a bitter cold January, she found herself in his tawny and welcoming arms. He sang to her empty caves and filled her hearth with pollen and seed. She felt the tapestry of him embroider her and fill to brimming her soul's flask. Her well within soon sprouted a meadow in which they dwelled in fragrant creativity.

And each spring, like certain other male canaries, this rhapsodist grew a new song, seeding their union with gardens of unseen flowers to be.

2002

VERONIKA'S INVISIBLE FINS

Veronika was known as the only mermaid who could make her fins invisible. Despite this ability, she would still be in danger were it not for the vigilance of Oliver Osprey, her beloved sentinel. This osprey of amethyst eyes and colossal wingspan kept a constant watch for humans, or hind-leggers, as he called them. Rabbits, squirrels, blue jays, hummingbirds, and other winged or four-legged creatures were welcomed to their island nest, but if a hind-legger were spotted, Oliver Osprey made sure Veronika was safely hidden from sight.

Veronika and Oliver Osprey had spun their sea-nest from the golden fabric of their inner selves. He was particularly adept at building their nest in a precise and mathematical way. As a mermaid, Veronika spun the aesthetics of words and images to create beauty. Together they made their nest their palace, and it grew larger and higher, just like the forests of pine, cypress, and oak that surrounded and protected them from the harsh winds and storms.

Being clever at creating structures, Oliver Osprey discovered how to develop a mountain lake for Veronika and her invisible fins. On his flights to the sea, he had noticed a vortex of currents churning below their nest. This whirlpool had only to be piped up to their mountain cliff, he surmised, and channeled to flow into a sunken area where a small lake had once existed. After a year or more of conversing with the migrant whales and dolphins, the visiting sea lions, and the indigenous birds, he finally discovered the way. He hired a hind-legger to install the tubing, plumbing, and other particulars. At last, Veronika, with her iridescent fins, could wander out in total privacy anytime she wished and swim in their private mountain lake above the seething seas.

This private lake was guarded by pines and cypresses, that dipped their ferny, gleaming fingers into the waters. Veronika would gaze through their lacy silhouettes at the wingéd life of the skies and the ever-changing cloud dreams. These amorphous cloud entities of enigmatic shape and sun-reflecting hues she named *The Fogarinos*.

It is said that Oliver Osprey would stand watch until Veronika, unseen after her lengthy, languid swims, safely reached their sea-nest. To this day, as a result of his vigilance, no hind-legger has ever seen the iridescent fins of Veronika. Only the Fogarinos, the squirrels, and other trustworthy creatures of tail and feather have witnessed them.

After all, if we don't protect what is vulnerable and unique, it may become an object of ignorance. Oliver Osprey understood this. Thus, he was among the wisest of birds.

1985

THE BEAR-CHAIR (MS. CHARE LITERAIRE)

There is now living among us a bear-chair. He is a brown, furry, and cuddly bear who walks on hind legs and drives a red truck. By day, he lives an ordinary human-like existence with his attractive Honey Bear of long, blond fur, gathering honey and doing some electrical jobs. But every night at 5:55 p.m., he vanishes from his bear-man existence and lives another life. Like clockwork, he reappears every morning at 5:55 a.m., before dawn, before his Honey Bear awakens.

So no matter how much Honey Bear may want to have a nighttime companion, she always sleeps alone in their rustic cabin. But she knows that as strangely as her brown bear-man vanishes, his cuddly, teddy self will reappear in bed next to her at 5:55 a.m. And that is how it has been for more than twenty years.

The most interesting part of this bear-man's life occurs during the evening when he transforms into Ms. Chare Literaire, a female chair, velvet-cushioned and voluptuous, with lovely, firm, purple arms. Ms. Chare Literaire is also an avid reader and prolific writer, reading and writing all night long with a fervor unknown to bears, chairs, or humans. Because she is strong, sturdy, and comfortable, she can read and write without moving from 5:55 p.m. to 5:55 a.m. every night.

At first, the Ms. Chare aspect of the bear-man found it impossible to read and be her literary self when Honey Bear sat on her. She became so frustrated having to wait for Honey Bear to fall asleep that she finally decided to contact other artist chairs to see if she could find a different space from which to work. She received a surprising number of responses to the inquiry she posted. Most chairs never reach out to other chairs, their arms being designed for other functions, but apparently there are plenty of lonely one-of-a-kind chairs. Anyway, Ms. Chare Literaire found an inexpensive basement to share with a stylish French barstool, an elegant Tibetan hammock, and a famous Roosevelt rocking chair.

She is relieved not to be sat on any longer. From her basement space, she can receive many manuscripts and movie scripts, along with her literary mail, and she sends out all she can of her own work.

Of course, she must be an incognito writer, as humans would never understand that she is part-bear and part-chair. Since she can never meet her own publisher, she pretends to be a female explorer who lives in Africa and is thus unavailable.

You may wonder, how does Ms. Chare Literaire get her mail out? Although he really isn't aware of his other life, the bear takes care of the chair rather instinctively. In the morning, when he is frying bacon for Honey Bear's breakfast, he eyes the letters of Ms. Literaire and makes a mental note to put them in his truck when he goes to town to sell his honey. Perhaps he is unconsciously serving his higher self, his true master. It's as if his bear-man life is fine and pleasant but sort of mechanical, his days a servant to his nights.

I won't bother to explain Honey Bear's confusion when she sees envelope after envelope addressed to many famous movie moguls and publishers with the name Ms. Chare Literaire written in the return address. But in the morning she is always so happy to see her cuddle bear again that her confusion melts.

It is said by a teenaged, long-eared owl who has observed the bear-man, literary-chair phenomenon, that this most unique, androgynous creature exhibits just the beginning of what humans will be able to do, not only consciously to recognize the multi-dimensional or parallel lives they already live but also to create clones from their myriad selves.

This young male owl also squawks that the most futuristic movies of the twentieth century have been produced by bear-man's chair, or Ms. Chare Literaire, as the humans know her; I mean *him*.

1985

A FIFTH SEASON

I'm living a fifth season
of an alien nature.
I hesitate and listen
for a familiar voice.
All need translation,
then fade away.

I wait in the strangeness,
the darkness of this alien nature,
to glimpse a profile,
a familiar curve
or recognizable scent.

But on into the lure
of timeless night
my soul wanders,
roots withering above the Earth,
grasping in the blackness
nothing of familiar turn.

Outside, the spring of nature
unfolds downy pods of bud,
petaled birds in wingéd bloom.

Inward, my fifth season wavers
amidst tidal winds of quandary,
yet moves on, a phantom
amid the outward spring,
in this my fifth season
of an alien hue, never seen before.

One boundless day, in late spring,
the ripening sun breathing me,
blossoming my cornered darkness,
I saw with eyes that could now see
a wondrous flower of myriad colors.
One petal was a mutant shade
of an alien hue, never seen before.

1985

130

THE MUTANTS' SPACE LOUNGE

It was all they could talk about. The people of Earth had never seen a creature so colossal of bone, so nimble of limb. In one step, this giant, Exo, crushed hills and flattened skyscrapers. Even though his feet were huge, they were like velvet, and his nature was so mellow that he would never intentionally destroy anything. In fact, on his home planet far away, he had been a sculptor who created glorious and delicate mobiles of ice from his breath. If he had known he was smashing art museums into oblivion with a sneeze, he would have left this planet immediately.

Curious to see what humans looked like, he had set out to find a certain cappuccino café on planet Earth. Finally, after days of walking about awkwardly, he heard disturbing voices coming his way and decided to abandon his mission. It was a relief to leave, because so far no place on Earth had been spacious enough for him. Humans still insisted on living inside boxes, which enclosed their heads, limiting their perceptions.

As he wandered on, he found himself approaching a planet where other creatures were more like him. At last Exo, the long, languid-limbed creature, happened upon a Space Lounge bustling with other mutants. This was the café he had searched for, the universal meeting place mentioned by the mutant pioneers he had encountered on his travels to other planets. Here the most exotic space travelers could gather and relax. Veronica could be seen with Oliver Osprey sitting on a stool that once was a colleague of Ms. Chare Literaire. Also, once a month on the full moon, the Lavender Bird Ears of the night could be seen suspended above love seats in a dark booth, cooing into each other's velvet-lined ears.

In fact, many of the amazing creatures that you encounter in this book have frequented this space lounge. Extra Vera visited from time to time, as did Intro Victor, who would often come for a bubbling spring-water. Because they loved to nestle and nuzzle, the Schnoozler Pets suppered in the most secluded corner they could find. They cozily hung out there three or four nights a week.

Even Fearita had made the trek once with Señor Past, before she had evolved into her present size, but because she was practically invisible, the waiters couldn't see her and therefore were unable to serve her. Their lack of response intimidated her and made her retreat. She vowed at the time not to return until she could become large enough to be visible.

Since the café was at the farthest end of the universe, no humans had ever dined there. The creatures that did come were all unique in some interesting way. Here, part-dolphin/part-humans would serve liquid delicacies in amber and moonlit crystal. And it was not unusual to look up and see a Fogarino drifting in through an open window, carrying diaphanous mist cradled in a rainbow goblet.

The Fogarinos were amazing to see; their voluminous, amorphic beings drifted in and would suddenly transform into defined entities with refined hands, fins, or paws that could steadily bring a glassful of themselves without splashing a drop. If just arriving from Tahiti, they might bring a fragrant tropical rain in one goblet and a mango sorbet in another. Other times they appeared pale and gray and were blue-handed with coldness as they carefully served the latest liquid version of themselves.

Not only had no human ever dined at this café, but none had even seen photographs or video footage of it. Being so distant from everywhere else in the universe, the café was able to preserve its own untrammeled realm.

The male bear's chair, Ms. Chare Literaire, had written about the café and its visitors in one of her movies, but the humans who watched her film assumed the space lounge she described was purely fictional. The movie had won the Science Fiction Award for the most original futuristic film. Ms. Chare knew that the film's popularity was partly because people were weary of being human and longed for the opportunity to experiment with being supernatural pets. Imagining oneself as a supernatural pet is like being an exo-terrestrial, uninfected by the generic stereotypes and limiting concepts of humans. One creature featured in Ms. Chare Literaire's film was based on an actual character called Howard the Duck, a benign and lovable pet. Enamored by mutants for his ability to embody both Earth and space realms, he became their liaison between worlds, quacking about his terrestrial experiences to whoever would listen.

The café had been founded by Langora, the pink, angora-furred mistress of Francisco, the purple bird-dragon. They had traveled together through the centuries in myriad forms until they reached this farthest edge. They had opened the space lounge so that, when in hyperspace, they wouldn't have to travel to the gravity sphere for cappuccinos and sugar fixes. Now these lovers only visited on their more sociable days to enjoy that rare opportunity to mix with other exo-terrestrials. Also, the whales, dolphins, and otters delighted in the exotic substances and camaraderie, bringing many an incredulous tale from their adventures in the global seas.

And the Giant Exo who had wandered about so awkwardly on planet Earth found continued enjoyment in the company of other mutants. Here, regardless of where their feet or fins touched, their minds were infinite.

1987

The Mutants' Space Lounge

WIDOWED FROM WITHIN

Yes, the dream and the way I interpreted it revealed everything. In this dream, he was married to an attractive Asian woman. Today, he and I spoke about how he was indeed beholden, but the marriage was not to a person—it was to his art.

I completely understood this, as I too am seized by a poetic devotion. In *You Alone Are Real to Me* by Lou Salome, I read that Rilke also was "widowed from within." This means to me that in order to be a certain kind of artist, the male and female of oneself must have the space and time to unite, separate, and then fuse in the mysterious act of creation. It's been said that there is no creation, only discovery of what is already there. For some, this mystery of creativity or discovery requires this strange widowing from within.

Thus, despite my attraction to him, I accepted his marriage to another, to his art, in the same way that I accept my own seed of destiny. And because of this acceptance, I feel resourceful and liberated, as if I have discovered a rare and exotic gem that I already know how to care for. After all, it could so easily be crushed or lost. Such delicate beings we are, he and I.

2007

A SILKWORM OF AN ARTIST

Consider the irony of a starving artist who unknowingly plummets the unconscious, then rises to the surface again for reorientation and replenishment. How peculiar that this type of artist can experience a kind of anorexia and bulimia, spewing out his artwork only after eating his own entrails, like a silkworm that is transforming itself into a white butterfly. So seldom has the world any green leaves to offer as nourishment that such an artist in a sense consumes his own creations. How rare are the artistic kin with whom he perhaps can nourish and inspire, finding camaraderie on those strange and solitary excursions.

2009

CITY HUNGER

Like a poet hunting for the most exotic metaphor, he tore into San Francisco. He ripped open the unsuspecting arteries of vagabond streets, thirstily drinking-in every bloody aspect. Then, like a villainous vampire with insatiable appetites, he drank even more, until the streets became as starved as he had been, and repelled him.

Finally, nothing was left but a kind of oblivion, a lust for what could never be, like a river that can't find its way to the sea.

2008

HALLOWEEN MUSINGS ON THE NATURE OF CREATIVITY

After weeks of arduous labor, seventeen paintings finally were birthed. What a relief to see them boxed and whisked away in a van to be framed. Wearing the masks of innocent faces, they had tricked and cajoled me, demanding perfection. Then, like leeches, they drank my last drop of blood, leaving me lifeless and drained.

Because of our symbiosis, it was easy for them to seduce me with their lines, colors, and textures. They took full advantage of my attempt to refine them, of my daimonic urge to translate impression into symbol.

Last night I was enslaved for ten hours, scrutinizing every detail with a magnifying mirror, until it was impossible to see anything, even them.

They didn't take their teeth out of me until today. Thank the lords they have departed and are about to be tamed in suitable frames, forced into new and separate identities, varnished and civilized. Such little cannibals some turned out to be. They began as innocents, gloriously inspired, and then, as if turned inside out, became their opposites, vampires, predators, demons—just in time for Halloween. Under the guise of art, they emerged to torture me, their creator.

I muse that destruction is an innate part of creation. And art, as life, is married to its own contradiction.

1996

A CREATOR

You bury your flames
in the storm-soaked earth.
And your heart turns
black, crimson, then gold.

Silver plums fall
from your mouth.
And your brown hands
beat the drum's belly—
sending music to the moon.

You think you're alone,
but you're surrounded
by your artistic progeny
who gobble you unmercifully,
using your body as mulch.

These little cannibals
birthed on pen and paper
make you a walking crucible—
a sacrifice to your art.

2007

THE GREATER IMPROVISATION

Captured by devils of distraction, I break out of this blur of poverty. I see through the world's crimes—the American dream, the recycled swindles of illusions, billboards of desire, marketplaces of flesh. And I dissolve, birthing an embryo, a mutant of my soul's hunger, redeemed. I am still a world-stranger, an exile, yet open now to the greater improvisation.

2006

AN EMBRYO EMERGING

As an embryo emerging
from a grim winter,
she faces life anew.
The bedraggled forests lie flat
at her breaking root.

In a time wrought with anguish,
when the sun is denied
and the stars become infidels,
she is reborn.

Is this what it takes to be a poet?
Is this a madness
the gods confer upon the innocent?

The shy dawn is not ready
for this shrug of word.
Only the gauzy fog proclaims her,
protecting her embryo
from human gaze,
keeping her, for the moment,
in the eye of innocence—
the honesty of water.

2010

PORTRAIT OF LISA FLEUR
part flower, part human

Lisa Fleur was lost, lost as a lily without a stem. Why was she lost? Where was her stem? Well, unbeknownst to the local humans, Lisa Fleur was in an interesting phase of evolution. She felt more flower-like than human, and the reason she became lost so easily was because she didn't care about the things that seemed to captivate regular humans. Lisa Fleur had a different orientation toward life.

Once she had a revelation which confirmed that the world she wove internally was that of a lily. Her body was more comfortable in her plant consciousness than in her human mind that represented the conditioned, the entangled, the mechanics of a militant will. She didn't like to memorize numbers, talk politics, or play with computers. She cherished the wild goats of the senses,[17] the adventures of hearing, touching, seeing, smelling, and feeling with all of her somatic being. Only the wonder of the moment's flow, the rhapsody of the tide's crest inspired her. The rest was fabrication, extraneous, the exhaust of the economic machine with its insatiable grasping.

Although her true home was a redwood cabin, the flower of Lisa Fleur's pantheistic spirit thrived in the wilderness with its ever-changing vistas uncorrupted by human politics. Nature offered colossal mountain bluffs dashing to the sea below, night's swirling galaxies, every pulse in infinite embrace. Tender fingertips of rain played musically upon her roof of petaled crown, filling her with song. Tiny birds twittered in the heavily coned pine trees. As the tides surged, so did she, currented by the Mystery. She was part of nature, another note of its symphony, in cadence with the wildflowers' dancing hearts.

When she felt too human, she didn't feel well or happy or imaginative. She needed to breathe in unison with other flora and fauna. When she tended to her petals, to the stem of her being, her diaphanous, flower-like skin became luminous, and her eyes danced with wildflowers and orbited with marigold suns.

By experiencing life through all the senses synergistically, the moment thrived in her cellular being, metabolizing her streams and rivers, becoming blood consciousness.[18]

From her roots, she emitted the musky fragrance of unborn nights. Even though she felt embraced by the radiance of the day's winter sun, the ebony night of her inner world with its insistent blood-urge bathed her in an invisible lake of emergence. Her tendrils drank of these transparent waters. Like a primordial creature, she gazed languidly through hazel, leaf-like eyes beyond all boundaries of physical limits. She could stay on the mountaintop above the sea and be involuntarily woven as a quivering thread into the endless tapestry of the cosmos. She could tune into the Mystery and be in wonder without going anywhere. By turning it all down, she was able to receive it all.

For many others, living this way might be depressing, a kind of dying. Without external distractions, some might feel desperate, their vacant souls haunting their every moment. For the white lily with the emerald green heart, the opposite was true. The magic keys to an Eden-like existence lay in feeling safe enough to be vulnerable and receptive, keeping a remote space to breathe creatively.

Nevertheless, it was challenging to be neither all human nor all flower. Recently her lily head felt separated from her stem. In an effort to be human, she had tried to live from her mind, but this severed her from her roots. Lisa Fleur simply wasn't interested in what most humans cared about. She had tried being human, had traveled extensively seeking new experiences for the wild bird of her soul, her heart's passions. These excursions usually left her feeling depleted, unfulfilled. Human interactions often involved egoistic scenarios. In her human mode, she felt disconnected from her greenness, from receptivity, vulnerability. When she lived from her plant nature, her emerald tendrils blossomed forth with possibility. She knew her roots to be a bulb of the infinite, not separate from the ebbing, surging core.

Yet how could she so easily forget the joys of the moment and sometimes feel like a lily without a stem? Only a flower-person would understand how this is possible, since the explanation is not logical. When one is a creature in harmony with oneself, with nature and love, there's nothing to think about or discuss. With the soft breezes carrying their jasmine scent and the clouds uttering their mute, lyrical language of images, everything is perfect without explanation, in an exquisite subtlety of existence, quite apart from the industry of being human. Through the timeless, sacred meadows, an unheard symphony resounds.

When senses are this acute, the most extraordinary bliss, including the miraculous, can emerge within the so-called ordinary. This heightened sensitivity makes everything possible. The gateways to heaven are opened. Infinity is our playground, and the exultance we feel illuminates every living plant and creature and continuously births itself anew. But if for some reason we are off-balance, we can no longer feel this joy. The senses are temporarily dulled. Yet if we protect and nurture them, they will revive as faithfully as the sun appears at dawn. We can trust in this mystery, even when our antennae do not realign immediately.

Lisa Fleur knew that life as a flower-person could be strange and precarious, but she accepted her nature, as this very sensitivity made the exultant possible. She had given up her will to the Mystery.

Yet, if it hadn't rained enough, if her stem was weak, if a thoughtless person had stepped on her, or if the winds had torn her delicate intricacy, she knew it was essential to withdraw and recuperate. During those times, it was easy to lose faith because she didn't have the energy to be brave, and that was where her beauty thrived, in the wild bird of the spirit. It was all part of being willing to risk herself, to find herself in ever-expanding vistas, to reach ever-more dimensional perceptions about the strangeness of the human world. To be willing to be lost requires much courage, but this was her path. Her marigold suns shone with this understanding.

Finally, roots unseen, Lisa Fleur arose, mesmerized by the exotic serenade of a rare bird perched on a nearby limb. Silence receded while the bird's trill resonated in the velvet chambers of space. And the fragrance of the day lived on.

2002

A DREAM COME TRUE

Yes, it was truly curious how he felt. After all, a dream had come true. Pablo had been working in isolation as a sculptor for thirty years, and suddenly he had been *discovered* by an international art dealer. He had once needed remoteness to be creative. But after three decades of working that way, he had become somewhat depressed. He wondered why he should continue, with such little demand for his work. It was art for art's sake, but it felt like only breathing in and never breathing out.

Miraculous sculptures filled his gallery. Over the years, a dispersed stream of friends and patrons had visited, and several even had fallen on their knees in admiration. Yet he had become so detached in his process that at times he even intimidated himself. One evening, wanting to free himself from his artwork, with bushy eyebrows flaring in maniacal fury, he proclaimed, "I shall burn them all."

Nevertheless, numerous collectors had purchased his sculptures, even though they were quite costly. There were masks, faces, and a few striking figures. One was a portrayal of Moses, another an allegory of the Seven Deadly Sins.

Now suddenly, out of nowhere, a sophisticate of the art world had entered his remote and private life, had promised him an exhibit at a prominent museum in New York, and had also promised to arrange an international tour.

Pablo was not as wildly happy as he had imagined he would be about his work finding wider acclaim. After the visit from the famous art dealer, he somehow felt a strange sense of loss, as if his world had been invaded and he had lost his independence.

Even if thirty years had been too long to work alone, that isolation had made it possible to bring the unique and masterful into a sterile and corrupt world. Perhaps the sacred was only accessible in the quieter realms.

A week after the dealer had left, Pablo's gallery of wooden images stood there silently reminding him of what he had once accomplished. He had done no sculpting since this intrusion. Would he be able to continue now that his intimate universe had been punctured? What good did it do to let his sculptures accumulate in his personal gallery? He had always wanted an outlet with the world—that was a lifetime dream. Although he had considered that perhaps he was too sensitive to deal with the art marketplace, it was still a fabulous opportunity, wasn't it?

It had only been a week. Surely he would be able to return to the passion of his creative world soon, he reassured himself. As he had done so many times in the past, he'd have to keep his faith that he wouldn't be abandoned by the Daemon just because his dream had come true.

It was a dream come true, wasn't it?

2007

THE BARREN WOMB WAITS

The barren womb waits.
Where will the next meal come from?
A tadpole or a kiss?

The muse has fled,
lost his face and perhaps his heart.

The barren womb waits,
somehow sensing
what will feed
its wanton hunger next.

Yes, the muse has fled,
yet is still alive,
doing other things now,
being with others.

The rainbows that hold the dreams
are still splendorous
and inspire the womb
with fresh visions and illusions.

As long as the sun and savannahs
of stars emit light,
the barren womb senses possibility,
and remains open to
the white fire of radiance—
impregnation by the Cosmic Kiln
with almost any form at any time.

2009

A SOVEREIGN PLANET

for Robinson Jeffers

Within your worlds of self, you walk about on two legs, as if a planet could do that. What kind of creature are you in your feral indifference? Are you set apart by your sapience, like a sovereign planet with its own red moon? Are you sometimes disgusted by what it means to be human, preferring the remoteness of the inchoate, detached from civilization and its corruptions?

Wouldn't you rather meditate in the timeless woods than be trapped in the industry of being human? Being so mechanical drags the spirit's wanderings away from discovery into tedium and habit. But you, with your soul strolling about on two legs, are drawn to retreat into the innocent black caves of revelation, letting your words flow from the ineffable.

2002

THE POETS' CRY

He peered at her
through the blue eyes
of clamoring skies,
his lips red and ragged
with savage discontent.

She stood there,
all moon, no sun,
shivering in the ravines
of no belief.

What stars had they
brushed aside to meet
so hungrily in the void?

And would the stars ever forgive
their brute sacrifice of mission,
or somehow understand,
like the moon understands the sun,
allowing its cheeks to be lit,
then abandoned.

The scarlet tongue of fate
cares not about these poets
as they work in the flaming darkness
while the elements race their pulse
to crest and to destruction.

Only ashes remain
of their poetic worlds
as they howl like love-wolves,
pitiful and trembling,
to the moon—unanswered.

2007

AN ARTIST'S IMPRESSIONS OF BIG SUR

While reading Albert Camus's "Portrait of Oran,"[19] I became spellbound by his ability to capture the town's essence, and thus inspired, I offer my impressions of Big Sur.

Gazing at the wild coastline, I see a world that breathes in equanimity with the timeless. Colossal cliffs dash down to the pristine sand and sea. With its paradisiacal peaks and its verdant forests raging to the ocean, why would this fecund wilderness need humans?

People plow roads, build cabins, live their lives, and then die here amidst the indifference of the eternal wilds. There is no coziness to this gigantic splendor, no intimacy in the remoteness. Here, only wolf-hearts survive, impassioned by the land, independent, and ruled by the moon. And in this toughening of spirit, characteristics are forged that offer humans a measure of their identity. Big Sur ignites a pagan celebration of its raw power and beauty; an almost inhuman element is needed to endure amidst the ever-changing and often ruthless climes.

A relief comes from recognizing and accepting the autonomy of Nature's laws, allowing their guidance. That humans can live and die here, not affecting this powerful land, is important to acknowledge, because from here we can discover our place in the greater order of things, rather than run our lives in egoistic ignorance, or in pseudo attempts at control. Experiencing the raw power of this land enables us to understand that we are conduits of the forces, of the Indestructible Entity. Dwelling here in a transitory reality, it is obvious that the wilderness spirit reigns with supreme majesty and can mercilessly erode whatever appears solid, plunging our cabins of plans to the sea, leaving us to contemplate the vacancy of our souls.

Indifferent to the purposeful residents living in the small tourist town nestled at the foot of lucid, screaming summits, the timeless grandeur of this dramatic coast caters only to its own cycles and seasons. Like the wild beasts that roam and slumber in the dense forests, this wilderness accounts to no one but its own eternal pulse, its own indomitable tyranny.

Here we may regain the innocence and connection to the Earth that once gleamed in the eyes of the ancients. When the tempests blow for months, these elements teach us who is really in charge. Humility is earned, and from there, a more graceful composure. Those second-home owners who visit on weekends may never discover the deeper laws that rule this rare and mysterious land, and probably would prefer not to. Sightseers observe the spectacular beauty of this raw country with an almost vulgar admiration, seemingly unaware of the violence that underlies and births this splendor.

Mountain lions, coyotes, and other species of wildlife roam, rarely seen. Reservoirs of silence in the vast solitude thrive, revivify life.

A miasma of cabin fever is also possible, as distractions are limited to a few hotels, restaurants, bars, small galleries, markets, a community library, the Henry Miller Library, and the Loma Vista Spirit Garden. Escapes to Monterey can be essential to preserving one's sanity, especially when the weather is inclement. I find Monterey, although a clean town, to be somewhat sterile and provincial, populated by numerous military personnel and retirees. Then again, the beaches are spectacular, white sanded, and the beauty and birdlife are wonderfully varied and abundant. The nearby cities of San Francisco and Los Angeles provide other amenities, including museums and other cultural pursuits. There also can be disorienting culture shocks at being cast into humanity's body.

Big Sur's lyrical shores resonate with the morphic fields of Greece, the seascapes and land described in the legends of Atlantis and Avalon. Like a rare, exotic butterfly existing on an otherwise chaotic planet, an accelerated power of transformation can work its way through individuals here. Big Sur offers a haven resonating with the origins of life, of the greater existence.

Endless, enigmatic vistas stretch out over the cobalt seas. The heavens mirror their lucid innocence upon the iridescent seas. On clear days one can observe dolphins and whales on their treks to Mexico, as well as fleets of pelicans and seagulls hunting and sunning in the tidal coves. Lone herons, condors, cormorants, swallows, falcons, vultures, and owls are also regular inhabitants. When one gazes at the mythical and primordial condors with their strange, bald heads and savage eyes, one senses the fire, stone, and oceans of creation and destruction.

Where can one find intimacy in such a remote wilderness? For some, with a lover or close friends; for others in a sequestered nook by the river, or in a shady forest's glen. And continuous is the invisible yet ever-present dialogue within.

The mysterious power of Big Sur has forged and blossomed a community of artists and artisans inspired by the fecund land, seascapes, and dramatic skies. Artists seem to sprout like wildflowers over the mountainous meadows.

Perhaps because of the nothingness so available, artists can pour themselves into this vastness, even if they remain unanswered by the stars above, the lidless mountain peaks, the unsleeping seas. Because of the remoteness, they can integrate the tangled skein of human threads, re-alchemize their experiences of this land's chthonic power, the sea's martyrdom, and survive in a curious way, amidst this small but closely-knit community of about fourteen hundred people.

Within this oblivion, the yoke of the finites balances the infinite, allowing one to gaze into the very eyes of existence, into the conflux of eternities.

Also, an isolation grip can force one outward to experience contrasting energies, people, and environments. One can feel as if one is vanishing because of a lack of worldly stimulation if isolated too long within the grandiosity of the Big Sur wilderness.

Despite the cosmic perspective that Big Sur offers, it only takes the arousal of survival instincts to be reminded of our basic humanity—especially when, after weeks of torpid fog buries the views, one can feel alienated and invisible. What was once a haven suddenly can become a prison from which to escape. During the winters, Highway One can be closed for months because of massive rockslides. One winter, helicopters had to fly in meals to feed the trapped residents.

This land invites a love-hate relationship because of its extremes. Temperatures can vary as much as fifty degrees in just an hour, and incessant, howling winds quickly teach detachment.

Big Sur appears to kick some people out, no matter how much they attempt to find homes, while others fit right in. Homes have become very expensive and scarce in recent years because of the prevalence of yuppies buying second homes. Previously, more bohemians and eccentrics lived in funky, gypsy styles.

Unpolluted and untrammeled, the Big Sur wilderness is among the few paradises left on Earth. It is also a kind of island or Noah's Ark that attracts a diversity of endangered species, including people, offering a refuge for many a fugitive to live out an odyssey with back turned away from a corrupt and invasive world.

2007

MYSTERIES OF BIG SUR

for Vince Clemente

From the foggy night,
a muffled sea roars
like an untamed beast
of the wilds.

Across the high-crowned
mountain range, lions prowl unseen;
their hides match the summer straw
they lurk behind.

Here, on this lost isle,
salvation is found, refuge
from the weariness of the world
in the gleaming nights and unhurried days.

As wispy mists
caress the canyons,
bathing the daisies,
a mysterious rebirth
quietly graces Big Sur.

2010

PORTRAIT OF A SPIDER'S HABITAT

Observing an expansive spider's web cast between boulders and facing a cascading waterfall, I chuckle at its awesome, sacred views, water chime music, and those sumptuous organic meals caught at home under the starry dome. What a pioneer this spider is, somehow to have crossed the impasse of river to achieve that precise spot—a tiny, sandy isle in the infinite universe. I marvel at the Zen-like aesthetics and savoir-faire he exhibits with such mindless abandon.

2004

A MASTER OF THE THIRD EYE

You appear on the stage of life as a magician—mirthful, quixotic, and adventurous, embodying the artistic passions, becoming more than life itself.

A photographer of life's fleeting images, you capture in your artwork and music what you see and feel through your third eye. A living master, you tear open the shady corners to light-beams of insight. As a Taoist, you are an unwitting orchestrator of the unsullied, exalted, and expansive realms.

O muse of my dreams, you discover the ultimate poetic places for our cherished walks, where our moments of whimsy fuse with the timeless sacred. What a confirmation of the elusive Mystery, that we have been drawn together.

Like Cocteau, you are a paradox, spinning ever fresh and contrasting realities as the very pulse of creation breathes and evolves through you. You play one reality against another, and in the shuffle, I see between the seams into yet another dimension. Your life is your art, not a thing apart. Thank you for existing, O Master of the Third Eye.

2009

THE MYSTERY OF CREATION

The last beams of the descending sun strike my back with heat and mockery. Immobilized by the anchor of so many untold secrets, I recline against a cliff-dwelling pine tree overlooking the cobalt seas. The vistas of no tomorrow insist I abandon myself to the vulnerable moment. Stumbling on into the eyeless wonder, I bathe in the life of suspension. This way of experiencing offers wings to the womb of the moment.

I emerge impregnated with the ocean's secrets, the unmentionable things—things disguised as puppy dog tails and lavender eyelashes. I ponder the irony of those who have eyes but no vision and those who are blind but can see.

Later, as diaphanous beams of a sapphire moon begin to veil my heart, obscuring my feelings, I wonder how to manifest this state of being. Taking out paper and pen, I am guided by the Invisible Current. Then I find myself entering my art studio and squirting tubes of oil paint onto oil-drenched canvas. I watch the colors fuse and dance, mirroring my secrets. I become lighter, and the sapphire moon laughs, lifting its beams from my heart. Then I see the moon depart, climbing a gossamer spiral to the vast dome of constellations, only to find another moon there. This one is Naples-yellow and belongs to Italy. Their heavenly light constellates—no war.

And I, who live for these moments outside of time, gather my swatches, my universes, caught like fish from an ancient sea. I carry them in and lay them all down, those lavender lashes and puppy dog tails. And the blind who stumble see again through their art. What will my mute images reflect in the dawn's transparent light? No judgments, please, I remind myself.

This work expresses the hieroglyphic codes from invisible worlds, cast out from meditative realms. My visual poetic language illumines my deeper existence, mirroring my soul.

2007

PICASSO EXHIBIT IN SAN FRANCISCO

Picasso, you have left your mark—
painting imagination's metaphors
with such brute force,
breaking all the rules
like an Earth giant, smashing
tradition and stale concept.

You crafted with the cunning
of a bestial sophisticate
the paintings the world so admires,
exhibiting a ruthless artistry.

You led like an extravagant giant
with your experiments, sublime.

Did you enjoy this strength,
this brute force?
Did it ever annihilate you
to be so bold,
so brilliant, so brute a force?

2011

CHAPTER 7
VISAGES OF DEATH

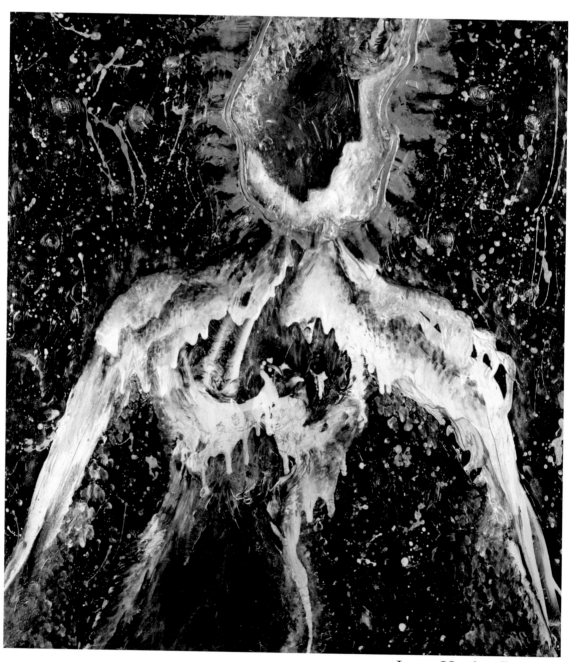

Laura Huxley's Departure

THE NEXT RHAPSODY

Ah, the leaf is quiet
in the shade—
only the wind's touch
moves it to tremor.

As it dries
to amber brown
and falls from stem,
the breeze dances it
to the sun's light.

And in its death
it comes to life.

Smiling, crackling,
it is sent ashore
on adventures unimagined.

And in the light
of breeze and day
it is tossed about,
then suddenly swept
to a cold, dark corner—
where it awaits
the next rhapsody . . .

1997

LETTER TO HERMANN HESSE

Yes, I too feel death nibbling upon my flesh—my face, my secret, muffled heart. What once was fecund is now hollow. The unbridled flood of so many paintings has exhausted my August of being. Like a fire that has burned down to a few mocking embers, I cry out to you, Hermann. Like you, I know that death waits. In fact, he feels so close that I can recognize his sunken, hollow eyes as my own. I can sense the force of his creeping, menacing shadow turning my flesh pallid, my well dry.

As you once asked, Hermann, how many lives are left? Why weep about the death that is just another version of life? I have loved so many and have ridden the horses of delight to the stars. I have blazed like a cathedral on fire. Why cry about the well going dry or the fact that my pretty bosom has nowhere to go but to its end, to my end. So what, I say.

Thanks to you, Hermann, I can feel the doom and dread of it all and the dauntless joys of my life still pulsing. You speak of what others shun. I am revivified thanks to your vow to drink from the moon's rivers and thus return with your masterpiece *Klingsor's Last Summer*. And this is my delivery from numbness and denial that feels worse than death. In gratitude to your bold, magnificent creation, my blood still throbs. My heart can still feel, and my bosom can still rejoice.

Reading your wingéd sorrow puts golden fish in my streams—singing to my soul. I join you in that eternity, dearest cadaver under the blossoming apple tree of sorrow's sun.

Yes, art is the only salvation. Thank you, beloved Hermann Hesse, for inspiring and reminding me with the splendor of your brave, exquisite confession.

2008

HER BROTHER PAUL

Paul had endured many a challenge. Early on, his father had unconsciously sought to destroy him through the savage and competitive instincts humans often display, especially toward the vulnerable and impractical—qualities epitomized in Paul.

But after a life of destructive habits and turbulent love affairs, Paul had finally found redemption in a raven-haired, strong-willed woman named Rebecca. Striking and capable, this woman doted on him, making him feel like a king. He was no longer a lost and alienated prince without a kingdom. His lovely wife had become the blessing by his side, offering him a devotion he'd never experienced.

But along with this blessing, as is true for many of life's gifts, came its antithesis—the curse of poor health. The thieves of illness ravaged his body relentlessly. He fought back with one life-saving surgery after another. And through it all, Rebecca cherished him, never leaving his side.

It appears that our most difficult experiences sculpt our character. This lost prince of yesteryear, this former Adonis, had through his challenges become an elegant man of valorous spirit. He never complained about his physical suffering and even managed to tell jokes and puns through it all.

Eventually, as a result of one of the surgeries, he became an invalid, paralyzed on one side. He was forced to give up his favorite activities, including tennis and fishing. Only later, after much therapy, was he able to walk with a cane. But these last years he couldn't take a step without suffering.

For many years, Cassandra, his younger sister, had felt serious concern for him. Despite the fact that she lived far away on a mountaintop above the sea, she always held a compassionate love for him. Somehow she felt his isolation, his misery. She carried his feelings within her as her child of compassion, like a mother carries her yet unborn. She felt what he didn't feel—was it even possible to be as pain-tolerant as he appeared?

The last time Cassandra and her lover Ramon had visited him in the hospital, Paul had proclaimed, "I'll be better tomorrow." But as he lay in a morphine-induced sleep, they both knew he was dying. The pallor in his face was alarming. Despite a year of chemotherapy and a recent report of a clean bill of health, his once-handsome face had become mottled, and the cancer had now spread to his back.

As Cassandra gazed at his close-to-lifeless form, she wondered what the unspoken part of him was saying. In the bitter midnight of his soul, did he feel the creeping claws of death grasping? Had death become the architect of his character, like the tyrannical father whom he had once struggled against? Had he internalized the savagery his father had formerly expressed toward his son's sporty, even reckless ways? Had the patriarchal systems continued to tyrannize him as they had earlier in his life, only this time through doctors with their surgeries, prescriptions, and chemotherapy? Or was it truly that an inborn vulnerability had originated in his acorn? Perhaps all of it was true.

"Don't worry, dear; I'll be better tomorrow," he had said. He didn't appear to know he was dying, but Cassandra and Ramon knew. During their visit he slept most of the time, yet drifted in for Cassandra's words and the touch of her gentle hand on his waning heart.

For a while, Cassandra murmured to Paul about her daughter's wedding and offered a few caressing words. Then, while he slept, she wrote her brother a note and quietly departed. They had stayed no more than a half hour. She and Ramon couldn't wait to leave the noisy city of lost angels. There had been bomb threats while they were there, and the city was chaotic, brimming with the static of so many people, cars, and cement. It was a world where busy-ness reigned. After all, they were used to living on the mountain cliffs above the sea, in the wilderness of their labyrinthine soul caves, in the kingdom of night's darkness. So, they couldn't stay in the city for long without suffering from a toxic overload, the annihilation of their once acute senses.

A few days after Cassandra and Ramon had returned home, they heard from the family that Paul was now in his last hours. They quickly embarked on what became a traumatic plane flight. At one point, the turbulence was so extreme that they were convinced their lives, too, were over.

Then when they arrived at the hospital, Cassandra was both shocked and distraught to learn that her elder brother had died just twenty minutes earlier. Their harrowing plane flight had coincided simultaneously with Paul's life-and-death battle. Perhaps that chaotic plane ride was a metaphor for the child of her compassion dying simultaneously with Paul. Despite the fifteen people in the intensive care unit fighting to save him, he had died in a violent struggle. His face held both the tension of desperation and the peace of final liberation.

It was difficult to recognize Paul in this body. Vacated, bloated, and lifeless, his body, like a hideous swollen fish, lay before her, stranded on the shores of a barbaric existence. She pondered the fact that once our spirits have departed, our bodies, devoid of breath, become useless, discarded cocoons.

Cassandra couldn't help but wonder if she was her brother's unspoken self. And what about *her* unspoken self? Did he know that she had this deep compassion for him? She wondered if she had spared him any suffering by carrying such empathy. How sick-hearted she had felt after his visit to her home four years before. How she had absorbed his isolation. But how much of what she felt was her own suffering projected onto him? Maybe Paul was the unexpressed part of *her*, the part she could only feel through others. All this time, she had thought it was *his* suffering, but perhaps it was also her own.

And now that Paul's physical, earthly form was gone, Cassandra was in dialogue with him, appreciating him in a new way. Why did it take death to spawn a more conscious realization of their bond? Why, Cassandra wondered, do we invariably take our loved ones for granted? And why is it often only when death comes to those we love that we discover the capacity for unconditional acceptance?

Their previous phone conversations were now sacred to her. Her beloved brother Paul had been so gentle, even protective in his last years. Their unspoken closeness made words quite secondary. Her once-lost brother, a prince-like Adonis with a wild wit and guileless innocence, had evolved through his experiences to become a king. How odd it is, mused Cassandra, that our destinies are played out by us as if we are mere puppets of their whim.

Her brother had died a hero to all who knew and loved him. And he left his baby sister, as he called Cassandra, many gifts in the form of revelations. Is that how relationship molds us, like a painting that mirrors the artist at every stage, continually demanding what it requires to be more complete? Perhaps we add ourselves to each other to make ourselves whole. We are each a unique current in the infinite seas of being, like inter-related DNA with fractilian connections linked together in endless cycles of birth and death.

Cassandra loathed the mausoleum where her brother was buried alongside their mother and father. How bizarre, she thought, this pickling of bodies, this burial in marble sepulchers. If you could peer inside those vaults and see the decomposing flesh, you would see what ugly surrealism humans have produced. Some people commercialize death and in fear of death make something distorted and expensive of it. And thus we become death's prey in yet another unnecessary way.

Cassandra's preference was to offer her body to the Earth, returning it to the Source through the crawling creatures, to the plants, flowers, and roots of Amanda, her favorite tree. But according to the authorities, this is against the law. It isn't permitted because it doesn't make money for anyone, she surmised.

Well, now Cassandra's child of compassion had been liberated through Paul's death, whether his earthly cocoon was locked up in marble or not. She reflected that neither his ancestors nor his enemies could clip his wings now; he was finally liberated. And in the rains of Cassandra's grief, her unspoken self had revealed itself as another treasured gift from the soul of her beloved older brother.

2001

FOR LAURA HUXLEY AND FRIENDS

So many feelings can't be expressed. Perhaps the most important ones must go unsaid. It seems that putting words to the soul's tremors can destroy their delicacy. When a beloved is dying, how intimate is our hearts' embrace. In the midst of these raw tides, we cherish the poignancy of every moment.

We are all dying, and being conscious of this sobering truth gives the moment its inherent wings. The passion of intimacy we can share with another in crisis and otherwise seeds our beings, changing us forever beyond what we can imagine. A mysterious exchange of gifts flows between caretaker and recipient, as loving reflections of each other.

It is interesting to examine the roles we play. Often it is possible to see the karma or seeds of being a caregiver early on in one's life. In the words of Mephistopheles, "In the end we all create the creatures we ourselves depend on." That is a thought-provoking statement. Certainly the shadows we cast are ourselves reflected, as are the rainbows.

As always, Laura made the impossible possible. I say this because the nobility and courage she lived in her dying gave me a strength that will blaze on within me as an undying torch. I am ever fortunate to have been inspired by the muse of Laura and to share her radiance with others.

2007

O ETERNAL FLOWER
in memory of beloved Laura Archera Huxley

O Eternal Flower,
how fragrant your scent
and how far-reaching your roots.

Although you've come and gone,
you're still here, nonetheless
Somehow, concepts of life and death
are too limited
for your present formlessness.

No, it's not real to me
that you've died.
It's no more real than
life's other illusions.

My truth is, O Eternal Flower,
that you still exist—outside of time,
a scent that forever lingers.

How infinite your spirit
as it travels the universe
and mocks the smallness
we dote upon.

O Eternal Flower,
how fragrant your scent,
how far-reaching your roots.

No, it's not real to me
that you've died—
no more real than
life's other illusions.

2008

GRIEF AS MY OFFSPRING

The infinite walls of night climb higher and higher like a tower of longing, while heaven's jewels tumble into the beseeching arms of silent, sentinel trees.

O waning, white moon, how vacant you are tonight in your barren beauty. Your mercurial beams cannot reach my cold heart. You linger in black shadows like my lover of long ago, whose arms no longer caress me.

Like you, my heart is starved and pale. Leaving only the evanescent froth of memories seeped in bitterness, my long ago lover has ebbed from my shore. His light, like yours, is seen as if from another planet; no longer are we one. And I, the pathetic human of this abysmal night, become smaller and smaller in my draining sorrow, my recent loss of loved ones. Nothing answers me as I let my wailing go to the seas, to the prospering infinity of the heavens. Everything becomes larger as I become smaller.

With grief as my offspring, the flesh of my glowing inner chambers trembles. On this lost night of the dead, I offer my breath to their rebirth, to the next form in the formless.

2002

A REBIRTH

I long now—only for myself,
for those ancient flowers
to return within—
to bloom eternally.

Yes, I include you, my Beloved,
in the buds that spume,
in the seeds that swell—
in this fragrance of longing.

For I have been wandering,
lost in the fragments,
in the seams between realities.
Even the moon has missed me—
so long have I been gone.

Yet the night
has consoled my cries,
holding and rocking me
in its fathomless arms,
where I am joined
by the lovers of all times.

Yes, I wait now
as the universal womb
waits for spring, remembering
my place in the infinite
after forgetting my roots
to the wells.

Having been broken
by the experiment of living,
I dangle from the cliffs
of the Aegean Sea,
only to be rescued by
the eternal rose of love: Eros,
who is also dying
and being reborn.

Suddenly a fragrant rain falls
and I blush emerald
in the dawn.

2008

EDMUND'S CABIN

Edmund, your cabin, the lair where you once dwelled, has become a living testament to your life. How fitting that this external womb where you created your masterful sculptures is gradually sliding from the cliffs to the sea below. Your Zen way of living is now being exhibited like a final living sculpture, in cadence with Nature's rhythms, the vast Mystery that moves what remains of your existence back to the primal waters.

On the eroding, earthen driveway are keep-out signs and gates, yet death and its guests cannot be blocked. Rats and other trespassers leave their dung in what once was your impressive gallery, your cave of invention. The tall, narrow cabin windows, shattered by Nature's forces into kaleidoscopic fragments, are now open to the sea's thrust. Swallows fly frantically in and out, building their nests in the old wooden rafters. And the once impeccable, yet indigenous gardens, released from your concepts of beauty, grow freely in their own wild season.

Where we used to lie long ago on sofas opposite each other, the rats now have parties. And through the planks in the floor, I see the jutting cliffs below. The heater, refrigerator, and propane tank have tumbled down to the water's edge. The wooden deck just above the sea where we once enjoyed our tea-sipping communes continues its fall into aquatic oblivion.

Yes, beloved Edmund, only the present moment is real. The rest is breaking open to a yet untold history, the Blazing Eternal.

2009

Edmund's Tree Song

MATTER CAUGHT, SPIRIT SOARS
in memory of beloved Edmund Kara

"Come, come," wailed the Mistress of the Sea. "Come to my violet churn of bosom, O King Spirit of the Sea. Let me unfold from the heart of thee, you who guard the primordial caves of the underworld spirits. Come lie down across from me upon old, velvet couches above the sea. Let me behold your sculptured being, your biblical visage, as the twilight gilds your creviced brow. Behind you, through narrow, tall-eyed windows, ships of the night pass distantly on a vanishing horizon. And I gaze, feeding upon you as you face the north and I the south. Blending our souls like larks in a summer dance, we soar in one rhythm of song. How I long to cross wing again with you, O Muse of My Blood's Leaf."

Instantaneously, as if in answer to her prayer, the Mistress divined a nimbus of quivering light enshrouding her. Resplendent with shimmering glow, she fervently sang into the dark depths of night's moistened seed.

"You wait for me, suspended between the veils of life and death, between the light and dark of worlds. As a deep-sea diver of silence's fragrance, you are the Muse of Unconscious Becoming. You answer my echo from the cobalt caves of primeval lament. You moan of your younger sister's suicide many years ago, and how you erected a sacred space in tribute to her phoenix rising. And here I am another sister of kindred soul, still on Earth, tracking your wild scent, like a lost and mad animal, entering your grave, pleading with you to re-inhabit my heart's flame."

The following afternoon, barefooted, the Mistress of the Sea walked with her prayer of longing to his discarded seashell of a lair above the sea. In the five months since his death, her beloved friend's possessions had remained untouched. Meekly beaking around them, she moved slowly, like a vulture devouring the memories they evoked. Then she entered the abandoned studio where the creations still emanated the powerful countenance of their creator—particularly Moses, which towered with nobility, embodying his sculptor's essence in every wooden fold.

Here, the abandoned cabin stood with his gallery of creations as if struck by lightning, caught in time, the spirit of him sculpted in wood, through the form of the Master who was now freed, released to the formless.

The aroma of her Muse-comrade lingered on, absorbed in the walls, in the old, soiled tapestry pillows. She greedily consumed his spirit's continuing richness. The burgeoning seeds of his pomegranate-self trickled down her throat like his blood, assuaging her soul's thirst for his essence.

"O Merlin of the Ocean's Treasures," the Mistress wailed on, "how fertile your ever-growing tree. How you flower from your death with fruits beyond the earthly orchards, released from the traps of concept. Your liberation has fed you more than life could continue to yield."

"O Seducer of Beauty, you bow down from the heavens, from massive branches silhouetted in the moonbeam's stare. Brimming over with red seed, you are as generous in your death as you were in life, giving all to your loved ones. O King Spirit of the Sea, you guided me through living example along this earthen path with heaven's reassuring hand outstretched from infinity. Behind the veils of death's black wings, your immortal heart lingers, consoling the sorrows of the hollow ones still breathing life on Earth."

"The Invisible, seen only by the Spirit's eye, roots the pulse of the visible," murmured the Mistress of the Sea, from her velvety caves in the holy silence of darkness.

"Memory is the white bride of the wedding with eternity," the Mistress added, chanting on into the night, as the Muse insisted she continue to ride his silvery wing.

Within the infinite flower of the unfolding petals of night, a fragrant lavender bud smiled to the sliver of silvery moon, whispering of the Master's immortality in his living sculptures, in his abandoned seashell above the sea.

2001

O WINTER SEA

I call to you, O Winter Sea,
to come and inhabit me
bringing your potent thrust,
your surge and trust.

Yes, come to me,
dark, daring lover deep,
and circulate my pale moon caves.
Sing to me
of your ancient strength
and fearless force.

Encircle me with your arms
of liquid devotion.
Let me find faith
in your throbbing pulse
that feeds my veins.

Yes come to me, my dark lover sea,
splash up my terrace steps from below
with bold and resolute wave.

Swirl deep and deeper still
into my sunless soul
and offer me your ancient rhythms—
the music that seeds the origins.

Give me that churn of blood
that rises waves to thrill.
Feed me your consistency,
your Will beyond will—
that bathes the sands
so ceaselessly white.

Yes, fuse your ancient pulse with mine.
And flood my thirsty caves
with your emerald roar.

2010

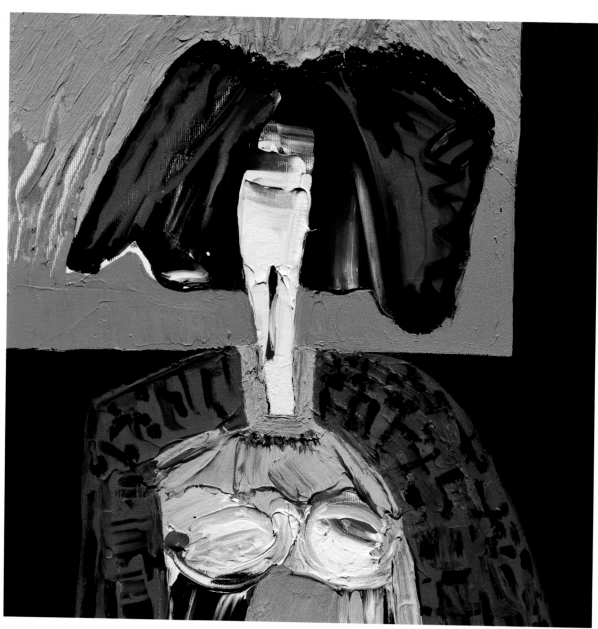

Under the Geisha's Mask

SUI-LAN

in memory of Frederic DeBraconier

Sui-lan and I had been close acquaintances for a few years before her untimely death. We had attended a meditation class and afterwards often shared thoughts at a nearby café. I was quite enchanted by her lovely mannerisms and whimsical sense of humor.

The kind of things most people seek came easily to Sui-lan. She was a protean spirit with an unusual intelligence and sensitivity, which made her exceptionally charismatic, personable, and lovable. A lyrical creature, she moved in graceful, undulating rhythms. She seemed, without knowing it, to exude the essence of humility along with intense strength. She had an ivory, oval-shaped face, with eyebrows, somewhat thick, arching like the dark wings of a dove. Although she had a fearless candor about her, her almond-shaped eyes were gentle and innocent, often gazing into the beyond—yet Sui-lan remained very present. People were magnetically drawn to her.

In utter contradiction to her illumined side, Sui-lan could, when using alcohol, suddenly transform into a hissing viper. This darker disposition, as she once remarked, was perhaps attributable to Mars ruling her rising sign. But later, I began to wonder if ancient, ancestral wounds were being enlivened.

Sui-lan was born in San Francisco, and her parents, who migrated from China as a young couple, kept their previous lives and heritage a carefully guarded secret. That could have contributed to a sense of alienation deep within Sui-lan. But who can say what wild force had driven her at the tender age of twenty-two to hurtle herself, strapped in her car, off the jagged cliffs, down to the fathomless abyss of the sea. What heartless power had so forged her soul?

Sui-lan's suicide brought me to an unquenchable grief. I've dug into the burrows of my soul attempting to understand what led her to such an intolerable state of despair. After all, she was in a budding stage of life and had the blessings of health, youth, beauty, intelligence, a loving partner, and other close relationships.

She also had a promising government job. But in this regard, she may have simply felt used by her gifts, for her job wasn't able to fulfill her more spiritual needs. In our café chats, she had complained of feeling like just another cog in the mechanical wheel of industry, an arena where the most aggressive psychopaths rule. In those oppressive systems, perhaps she sensed that a reconnection to her ancestral roots and a reconciliation of spirit and matter were inherently impossible, that more expansive possibilities for fulfillment might only be found in living outside of consensus reality. Sui-Lan never had the chance to aspire much beyond the economic necessities.

Her lover, a third generation American, may not have been capable of understanding her, of helping her synthesize her ancient roots with contemporary reality. In many ways, I think, she felt trapped between worlds. For deep in this young woman's cells stirred all the fascinating though obscured legends of her Asian heritage—Confucius, the *I Ching,* superstitions, mythic dragons, reverberations of the zither, ancient masks and dances.

Her cellular inheritance also included a darker history, the foot binding of infant daughters. What could possibly have seemed charming about those disfigured feet or the uncertain gait that resulted, those arms held out from the body, that slight inclination of the body almost abandoning itself to chance, subtly suggesting hesitation and distress. This ritualized primitivism was designed to make men feel more powerful by ensuring the helplessness of women who could not be steady on their feet.

Perhaps in Sui-lan's eyes, little had changed; after all, women are still making similar sacrifices today in the myriad roles they are willing to play, and in engaging in a kind of mutilation through the practice of plastic surgery. Did Sui-lan's suicide symbolize an archetypal sacrifice for all oppressed women, ancient and contemporary, who haunted her soul? Could it have been an unconscious attempt to transmute the suffering of all women, if not in the torturing of their bodies, then in the squelching of their potentials?

Also, her ancestry included the victimization of the Chinese by the British, which sometimes caused a "black mania,"[20] a wailing and foaming at the mouth of the "coolies" who periodically reacted like injured, enraged beasts. Perhaps on a deep cellular level, Sui-lan had a blood consciousness[21] about all this. Her sensitive nature could have made her more vulnerable to the cries of her ancestors, driving her more deeply into despair, imprisoning her with the invisible burdens of her labyrinthine soul. In fact, if one were seeking meaning in her tragedy, one could say she died from an archetypal affliction.

Perhaps the forces that contributed to her suicide can never be resolved, but a few weeks following her death, I had two mysterious and uncanny experiences that brought some measure of peace. One evening while I was swimming in my pool above the sea, an image of Sui-lan appeared mischievously riding on the red tail of Mars as if to remind me of the comic tragedy called life. The dazzling star she rode illumined a path before me on the dark waters. There we met in synchronicity, our hearts in communion. In a dilated moment of epiphany, she revealed not only her whimsical side but also the unbounded glory of her liberation.

A few nights later at my pool, as I gazed into a candle's dancing flame, the essence of Sui-lan magically re-appeared. As our hearts merged and expanded in the strange eternity of white light, connecting to the rhythm and resonance of all creation, I began to weep.

When my tears abated, Sui-lan silently murmured, "There is no death; our souls are one in the eternal bond of light. Whenever you reach for me, I am here with you, only a membrane away."

I trembled at this mysterious red dawn arising, and with deep gratitude felt the divine weave of reconciliation.

2005

EMERGING, YET TREMBLING

All is exultant in
the river's mad rush,
as the Sublime cascades
into waterfalls of song,
carrying mortal things away.

Dead trees spring to life,
swaying in the frenzied currents.

Grain bursts, thrilling the meadows,
and tiny, purple wildflowers
peer silently into my eyes.

My own presence
mysteriously prevails—
beyond the midnights of the soul,
emerging, yet trembling
in the new dawn's glow.

2011

MUD IS YOUNG AGAIN

Mud is young again. Long-dead tree trunks roll hysterically to oblivion in crazed rivers dashing to infinite seas. All is lost and regained in the river's pulse. Beginnings gurgle from mossed sacrifice after the storm's assault. Muddy waters converge while twilight, weeping on ecstatic knee, creeps in. Frenzied voices of naiads astride the river's bucking crest laugh wildly, freed to be reborn in the seas of death.

2004

THE DEAD ONE IN DIALOGUE WITH THE REMAINING ONE

"What is the difference," the Dead One asks the Remaining One, "between you and me?"

"Well," answers the Remaining One, "for one thing, I still stalk the Earth, the windy sands of today's beach, with a passionate heart."

"Well," says the Dead One, "how do you know I'm not there, within your bloodstreams, in your pulse? I don't need to be visible to exist, do I? Can't I live through you and thus be as *real* as you?"

"No," replies the Remaining One, emphatically. "To be truly alive, you have to be embodied and pulsing in the flesh. You rapaciously leech vitality, passion, and desire from my wells without invitation. You, in fact, seem remarkably comfortable usurping me," retorts the Remaining One. "But that doesn't make you *alive*."

The Dead One answers indifferently, "You would hardly exist without me. As an ancestor, I fuel you. It takes my ambitious urge to thrust your work outwards. You wouldn't be a playwright or philanthropist if it weren't for my unrequited thirst embodying you."

The Remaining One impatiently counters, "Perhaps! But what you are saying is not new, and I'm sure it's been better said. Be quiet and let me bask in the sun's insolence a while longer. Just because I'm facing abrasive gusts of wind on this beach doesn't mean you should add to the assault. I see no difference between you and the brute forces. So I will attempt to accept all your forms of existence. One thing is definite: I do not eat from the same platter as you, except when I am distorted enough to prey on my own entrails, which unfortunately happens often these days when I'm weary and lack the energy to imagine or wander. Speaking of eating, O Dead One, what food do *you* offer? Stale nostalgia, dry bones, white ashes? That is your pitiless and pathetic palette of leukemic sheddings. We can't offer more than what we are, can we?" the Remaining One smirked.

"How self-absorbed you are," exclaims the Dead One. "You might as well be me, with all your eccentricities and your back to the sun. But I will let you know that I prefer your compassion to anything else about you." The Dead One smiles palely. "Yes, your compassion is more delicious to me than the rest of your menu. If it weren't for that, I'd have little of you to consume. The tyrant of you is a blazing farce, the fool of you overplayed, the queen of you an anarchist. All of this leaves cold French fries at my back door. I don't even *like* you," adds the Dead One contemptuously. "You are as close to dead as an embodiment can be," he adds chuckling, "and still be called alive. The sustenance I derive from you is so minimal that if I didn't enjoy fasting, I would abandon you."

Staunchly facing Death's void stare, the Remaining One calmly replies, "You won't abandon me as long as you can find something of me to devour. And compassion is a most rare and delectable essence in our decadent times. Else, you may not need me, since there are innumerable others on

Earth whom you could inhabit. Yet I sense that you will continue to reside in me for now. After all, the nourishment I provide gives breath to your otherwise nonexistence."

The Remaining One adds, "I also recognize that in the human catastrophe, you romp like a wild and invincible chimera. Perhaps there are planets where death doesn't need to *be* for life to exist. But here, you have a vast playground for your gymnastics. And I must say you're certainly exaggerating your power in the escalating suffering, bloodshed, and violence. Will you ever let up? Or does the overpopulation of our planet simply offer you too many parts to play, too many opportunities for your cannibalism and will to power?"

The Dead One stops for a moment in the timeless vacuum, as if he'd heard enough.

The Remaining One continues to ponder their dialogue. What would happen if she *were* less compassionate? Would she be saving or selling her soul? Would this Predator starve and leave her stronger? At the very least, would she live longer by entertaining death less, or are mortality and immortality lived simultaneously?

Eventually the blood of the Remaining One grows pale, weary from the onslaught of unanswered questions. So when the last flicker of the blazing orb descends behind a craggy boulder, she feels relieved to run barefoot through the tides.

Another day is about to be extinguished in the encompassing twilight, and with it the compulsion to create. Another day of birthing is about to end.

2004

A CONSUMING BRILLIANCE

Twilight eases the cries of day,
softening ragged bluffs within—
then, carried by night's rapture,
is lost to the black womb of seed.

At the savage cove below
where the ocean seethes,
wild things fold their wings
in the night's dark shadows,
sleeping in spirit-caves
alongside the fleeting tides.

Then, over the mountain's crest,
the sun's breath emerges,
banishing dawn again,
with a brilliance consuming
all that has been . . .

2001

CHAPTER 8
EPIPHANIES

Priestess of Dawn

IN THE MIDST OF MYSTERY
for Dylan Thomas

Sequins, strawberries,
the cracked moon . . .

Bowing to the worms
behind the masks,
I watch as skulls drift
on a silvery path
going nowhere.

The darkened, mute forest
tunnels my soul's cries.

Listening to that
which is of no man,
I climb the chords
of your flute's song.

Your passion's music
guides me with invisible hand
to a choir of pale angels
on their knees.

From there we travel
the infinite spirit of things
to the edge of all melody.

Then dangling over the abyss,
beholding endless horizons,
we are swept
by a crimson wind,
back to the origins
of all lovers and demons.

There we pause,
in the midst of mystery . . .

2004

THE ODYSSEY OF SELENE

It had all begun with the miraculous event of being born, the first breath of life's bounty. And tonight, the epiphanies continued in the full moon's flowered splendor as Selene swam in the warm, black lake with her lover-muse Ovid, her god of poetry and music. Emerging from the silver, moon-drenched lake, Selene lit a candle that symbolized the passion of her golden spirit offering light to the night's kingdom. It was a metaphor for the life of imagination and spirit, for the isle of her dreams, a self-created Ithaca, a Garden of Eden above the sea.

Selene knew that to consider anything as self-created was illusionary—for she recognized that her personal myth was seeded by the cosmos. Nevertheless, she felt called to transform matter into spirit through her own unique style of being. As a conduit of the sublime, she offered herself to the River of Life, metabolizing and spilling the blood of experience and revelation into her poetry and art.

After reading, studying, absorbing the life and work of Nikos Kazantzakis, Selene couldn't help but draw comparisons. She recognized the stature of his work to be monumental, while she considered her own to be that of a minor figurine. But that wasn't the point. What mattered was their mutual quest. Her soul's thrust shared its thirst with Nikos and other heroes of the spirit.

Over twenty years ago, she had retreated to a mountaintop. Her drive to shed society's prescriptions had gradually dissolved much of her conditioning, re-alchemizing her being.

Selene thrived when in dialogue with origin, with the elements, with Ovid and the music of his primordial soul. For her, the night's starry necklace strewn across the midnight dome, a blazing fire, the whirring sound of the hummingbird's wings, the pink-blossoming almond tree, and the solitude that nourishes the senses were life's most precious jewels.

Her memory was not for accumulating data or historical facts but for experiencing life somatically through the wild goats of the senses.[22] With this sensibility, she could offer the altar of her soul's most receptive vulnerability. Perhaps, Selene pondered, the type of memory we have determines to a greater extent than we can imagine who we are and what we do. So many borrow their work from history, from others. But with memories that do not feed on history and imitation, artist-visionaries emerge, constellating other orbits, discovering from a mysterious inner magnet, which uses them unmercifully. Their suns and their shadows are as beacons drawing them in, exploding them out through their creations as other stars being born. Through this organic process, rather than becoming redundant reproducers of stale realities, artists are liberated, becoming true innovators.

Selene envisioned herself re-igniting the Elysian Mysteries in her way of living, restoring the origins of the Garden of Eden at Pankosmion,[23] above the resounding seas. In that desire toward the simple, the fusion with the untrammeled world, she was devoted to seeing behind the mere appearance of things, to collaborating with the invisible. Contrary to the acceleration of homogenized, insatiable consumerists, her path was propelled by a need for transformation and freedom. She was an anarchist behind the scenes, renouncing misdirected desire.

Selene was drawn to what others ran from. She thirsted for nothingness, longing to be the empty avatar awaiting the unknown. She had little personal will, just passion. She was nonchalant about the world's distractions. Sublime symbiosis, infusion with Otherness was her mystical seducer. She needed to ascend the everyday mechanics of mortal existence whenever possible. Her passion was to study the flame behind human behavior, observing and deciphering the innumerable masks, penetrating the dynamic energies of the cosmic forces and their ruthless use of human beings as tools. She felt, as Nikos Kazantzakis said, "It isn't man I love, but the flame that devours him."[24]

Ovid's brown, primal hand rested on her white, curvaceous breast as she wrote these thoughts, "I want to rid myself of excess in mind, body, possessions. The monk of me needs to withdraw, to fast from what others desire, to be One within the meditative moment, to inhale freedom's breath."

Ovid had fallen asleep earlier that evening as she strove to write what felt like paltry words. That night she felt her inadequacies, and that was acceptable; she recognized they were merely symptoms disguising the Predator's relentless nibbling. With that insight, she could observe rather than identify with that state of mind.

She would use all of the Tao's ingredients, whether pleasant or not, to delve into the world, into herself, more extensively in a self-fashioned dialogue with the universe and others. She understood that the curse spawns the blessing—that the seed of life coexists with the seed of death. She could now embrace death as a protagonist of life. They weren't in opposition, as she had once thought. She would use all of life as the clay for her spirit's flame, however impermanent.

Selene recognized that human behavior is fueled by our animal instincts and that sometimes we must struggle to transcend the bestiality of these impulses. With a simpler, more distanced understanding, she resolved to observe her enemies, those who confounded her blood's flow. She would study them as reflections cast onto the lake of her mind, revealing more of the Mystery's forces. She would consider how much of her experience was her own projection and how much belonged to others. Wasn't it all the micro of the macro?

It was time to be reborn, to rid herself of useless illusions and the toil they caused. An intolerance hovered above her like a torpid, gray cloud. The outside world offered little, except media for discovery and expression, grist for the soul's mill. The many phantoms of seduction and distraction had already revealed their faded, worldly faces.

Perhaps she was really drawn underneath it all, below the simple joys, to a kind of death or void, the primal well from which night's seeds are spawned. From there, the Mystery, her true lover, consistently murmured to her. The spirit of all she experienced, studied, and reflected upon ceaselessly re-alchemized her blood, like tides ever breaking upon the shores. And Selene was irresistibly drawn to live and work from the realm of the unconditioned. She longed to be the deep-sea diver again who explores the unknown, returning with new treasures, untarnished gems.

Convention validates the competitive ambition of the individual to surpass even one's own self, while Selene felt the opposite. She had brushed aside the outworn drives and illusions, like the dry straw of summer grass. One must become a god-slayer, an anarchist, and retreat in order to live freedom's pulse, she soberly surmised.

"Never shall I bend and bow down to that senseless dark which blots out the holy light of man," said Nikos in his *Odyssey*. Let us ever "seek freedom in a ruthless, sleepless strife." Selene also felt this call as her own soul's cry. Although she knew she was a different alchemical mixture than Nikos, he was able to feed the ineffable to her soul. She would continue to succumb to her "introverted frenzy," as Nikos termed this possessed way of being in his own life.

Further, Nikos wrote that when the mind marches "beyond all sorrow, joy or love, desolate without a god," there follows "those deep, secret cries" that pass "beyond even hope or freedom." And there thrives a "godless and hopeless world."

Prevelakis, the beloved friend and collaborator of Nikos, wrote, "These thoughts may not bring about peace and joy. One may act like an automaton. Yet in the exultation of Nikos' passionate nihilism, there is more air to breathe." And from Nikos, "Don't say you have paid dearly for this deathless flame. Deny appearances; follow your own vision. The ungovernable world is a transient fantasy of the human mind…. There is no master now on earth; the heart is free."

Other thoughts that Nikos aroused in Selene included the Freudian idea of slaying the primordial father, and at last, God, with the world's dream being the final temptation to overcome. In addition, he pointed out that rationality is incapable of penetrating the Mystery, but he also acknowledged that mind is the "great master that crafts man from the homeless air."

These liberating insights of Nikos inspired Selene, strengthening and answering her deepest longings. She yearned to be free of the thorns of existence. The mirror of delusion had been shattered by what it meant to work in the world. And she had been wounded in the process. Now, the mosaic of broken glass was to be illuminated, each piece seen through as a window of reality, then swept away onto the ocean's floor, left to incubate for eons, then, with all human contamination erased by time, eventually re-found as wild gifts of nature's treasures.

Like the wind blowing out a thief's lantern, the mind can snuff out all memories. All things will vanish eventually. "Absolute in its essence, placed outside of time, unaffected by the contagion of the pitiful world, song consoles the nihilist in his solitude." As Selene rewrote these words of Nikos, she felt the reverberations of Ovid's song notes. "The only deathless flame is man's own gallant song," as Nikos said. In the other room, Ovid strummed his guitar and sang as if answering the echoes of lost, ancient worlds. Ah, echoes for the soul's cries, at least for the moment, here at the mountaintop nest of golden eagles.

Selene was deeply grateful to Nikos for inspiring her own odyssey, her imagination's Ithaca. This odyssey had re-formed her now, nourishing her essence, illumining more of herself to herself, thus deepening her understanding of the universe.

The sun had silently vanished behind the horizon, leaving dancing wisps of flesh-colored clouds. In the balmy breath of this late winter day, the cobalt seas appeared Mediterranean. Myriad birds twittered, settling themselves down to nest for the night. And Selene thought it all quite amazing that she and Ovid dwelled on such a mountain peak surrounded by the lyrical tides, the vast, seamless heavens, the seminal wilderness of their Ithaca.

At twilight, as she gazed upon the sunset-complexioned ocean with its ever-changing countenance, she thought about the unseen chaos beneath the surface, and the struggles and joys in her own life, some of which had risen to embody miracles. With all the tribulations, Ithaca was still her heaven on Earth, within her soul reflected.

How had these miracles happened? Life seems to live us without permission, mused Selene, as she wrote the final words of this story.

2002

OBEISANCE TO THE MOMENT

Down below, the sea sobs
upon thirsty sands.

Above, ancient beacons orbit
the ebony oceans of night.

I gaze in wonder,
aware of this transitory existence,
shedding my extraneous garb
in obeisance to the moment.

Dawn will come, oh so soon,
and sweep away
the enshrouding darkness,
yet unseen stars
will ever cast their ancient light.

2010

LAVENDER BIRD EARS ON THE ISLE OF CANDALABRA

According to the elves, pixies, gnomes, and other panhumans that dwell on the isle of Candalabra, it is possible on full-mooned nights to glimpse Lavender Bird Ears flying through the skies. What—one might ask—only the birds' ears? And the creatures that nestle in the vast woodlands would nod in unison and point across the snowy seas.

"Over there," they motion, "when the full moon casts its beams, the Lavender Bird Ears of velvet-lined gossamer can be seen, iridescent with beauty, drifting across the mercurial plains of an undulating sea." A fiery-haired elf with his long beard of red and purple polka-dots added, "It is said that these ears are the materialized spirits of the most exotic, oracular birds ever to exist. For only the wisest of birds come here to sip immortal life, flocking from all over the universe to this isle, where a rainbow of ruby, amethyst, and amber moons constantly radiates. On the resplendent beams of these myriad moons, their traveling spirits are carried to infinity."

Suddenly, a gnome began to sing their anthem.

"O Lavender Bird Ears of the night, we see you flying with iridescent lobes reflecting the lunar beams. We see the silky gossamer that lines your ears, so warm and fuzzy in the coolest night. Some can't see you. Others say you are flying saucers, but we Candalabrans recognize the Lavender Bird Ears of the night. We can see your furry velvet and can sense your oracular spirits."

And all the other creatures appeared entranced. They stopped singing and stared from their mountain crest across the cool winter seas. "There," one whispered, "do you see it—I mean *them?* Of course you never see just one ear—they are always in pairs."

I gazed into the snowy pale iridescence of the winter's full-sailing flower and glimpsed the Lavender Bird Ears of the night, their shimmering wave of gossamer rippling across the ebony tides. Awed, I felt honored to be one of the rare few to witness this spectacular sight.

1986

BERNADINE, THE BUTTERFLY

Bernadine, a blue-eyed butterfly in her teens, braided her long, blond hair over her wings. Suddenly, she found herself faced with a great challenge. An insensitive young boy had injured her mother by trying to trap her in a net. With a damaged right wing, her mother could no longer fly.

What was Bernadine to do? She remembered hearing once about a legendary doctor far away who was renowned for healing butterflies with torn wings. He was an ancient, gray, hairy moth who lived on a red gossamer throne in the middle of a spider's web that he had captured some time ago. According to local lore, the only way to obtain his rare and magical elixir was to climb ever so carefully up the perilous web and request it directly from the famous doctor.

Whereas her father, gravely concerned, no longer had the strength of wing to embark upon a strenuous journey, Bernadine fortunately had great reserves of energy. Determined to accomplish this task, she prepared for her journey. She put on purple tennis shoes and for good luck borrowed her father's favorite handkerchief. Inside it, she packed a peanut butter sandwich and one black olive.

She knew how hazardous an old spider's web could be, and she was scared. Her mother was hesitant to let her go, but with her wing in a sling, she kissed her courageous daughter farewell.

After Bernadine had flown for some time, she heard a thunderous noise and watched as lightning ripped open the sky. Quickly hiding under the trunk of a fallen tree, Bernadine nibbled on her peanut butter sandwich. But, too excited to be hungry, she re-wrapped the sandwich, the olive, and flew on.

Suddenly the sky began to cry more tears than she had ever seen. Poor Bernadine's wings became so wet that they stuck together and she couldn't fly. She tried repeatedly to lift her wings, but she couldn't. Her tears of frustration and exhaustion joined those of the heavens until she fell asleep in one large puddle.

When Bernadine awoke, the sun was shining brightly and the day was clear and warm, so she tested her wings. The sun had completely dried them while she slept. So off she flew, encouraged, determined to complete her mission.

Before long, she came upon the great entity, Dr. Moth, sitting upon his red velvet throne suspended in the center of the largest spun web she had ever seen. Many insects had been stuck in the web. She wondered how she would ever reach the doctor without becoming snared like the others.

Knowing not to step directly on the sticky strands, Bernadine first threw down her father's handkerchief. Then, careful not to slip, she climbed the web like a ladder, step by step. Along the way, she freed a ladybug and a fly.

After what seemed like an eternity, she reached the imperious throne of the famous Dr. Moth. He was snoring—his snowy mustache seesawing up and down. He opened his mouth and, with the messiest gust of a sneeze, blew poor Bernadine off the web and back down to the bottom.

Undeterred, Bernadine worked her way up again.

"Pardon me, I seem to be catching a cold," Dr. Moth said. "What can I do for you?"

Bernadine, offering her most gracious curtsy, pleaded, "What is the secret, kind doctor, to healing my mother's wing? It is badly torn, and she cannot fly."

Dr. Moth wiped his nose, then reached into his pocket and gave her a thimbleful of his secret balm. "Don't spill this, not even one drop," he cautioned emphatically. "This is the last of my supply. This and only this will mend your mother's wing." Bernadine bowed again and again, thanking him repeatedly, as she began to depart.

She knew the only way to carry the magical balm home safely would be to balance it on her head. Using her braids as ropes to secure it tightly, she prayed that no winds or rains would come. Flying by the light of the smiling moon, she arrived home at last without losing a drop.

Bernadine immediately gave the sacred balm to her father, who carefully applied it to the torn wing of her mother as she rested on the couch. After waiting patiently for the elixir to dry, Bernadine's mother flapped her wings several times and was immediately ready to fly again, circling their home. Elated, she took off through an open window for a flowering meadow nearby.

"I can't thank you enough, my dearest Bernadine," she said, fluttering her eyelashes softly against her daughter's cheek in a butterfly's kiss of deep gratitude.

1955

BLACK GOATS TURN TO WHITE

after the 9/11 attacks

O night, you turn your back to me, denying me the sleep of angels or mortals. I stare with open lids beyond you, reaching for the guidance my dreams reveal. There I envision, wandering beneath the purple heavens on the rolling mountains of sun-bleached earth, a shepherdess of long, green hair with moon-touched breasts and star-filled eyes. With this numinous creature is her herd of hungry goats searching amongst the grainless autumnal fields for what is not there.

She sings to her flock as if she were a diva of the nightingales. Her strange, wild songs drift through the air and feed the goats in another way than would the grain they seek.

All night the priestess sings to her companions, as if she expects the black goats to grow wings, to become other than they are in their needs of the flesh.

When she lays her long, green hair upon a mound of earth, the goats nibble on her locks as if they could turn her hair to grass. She merely laughs and sings another song, hoping they will stop and succumb to sleep.

At last the dawn casts its lavender hue o'er the mountain shoulders; the black goats fall asleep, and the priestess too is dreaming. She dreams that her goats don't need the grain now hidden beneath the soil, that their bellies will be sated by the songs that fill their hearts. She dreams that humans lose their need for war and no longer kill for food.

When the shepherdess awakens, bathed in the dew of dawn, she sees wildflowers growing all around her, borne before their spring. The flock of black goats has turned white, and each one sings to the others, politely taking turns. What a gentle herd. Even when singing in unison, each has a unique trill born from spirit's core. Beneath each cleft of toe, yellow daisies sprout from song. And the world has changed.

O night of dream, you force my true wakefulness and have offered me this flight of wing, this transitory peace from the anguish of the world. Perhaps now, with folded wing, my heart can sing within your gilded chamber. And now that other sleep, which had so eluded me, murmurs of the new world to come, the realm of soul-music that seeds a spring in winter, the blaze of love's flame that knows no human bounds.

At last I fall into an angel's sleep, my lost tears joining the growing rivers of human sorrow, the shores burgeoning with orchards of tomorrow's seed.

2001

THE FALLEN STAR

for Hermann Hesse

The heavens were black, pregnant with the night. Constellations of beckoning galaxies glittered from worlds unknown. Sabrina, the panhuman, with her white, willowy arms, swam in the dark lagoon of a moonless midnight. Shooting stars, burgeoning with promise, fell through the empyrean dome. It was as if Sabrina were waiting, waiting like a nocturnal animal for something to happen. But for what?

She wondered if she would ever feel comfortable in the world amongst the smiling façades, the slick, hi-tech fragmentation, to be an innovator amidst the homogenized contagion. She contemplated whether ethical or spiritual realities even exist in our terrorist-driven times, apart from the myths we create. Certainly she was familiar with appearances switching into their opposites, within herself and others. Who then are the next predators waiting to feed upon our spirits, she asked herself, and who are the next angels? And don't they coexist? Isn't it relative as to how much of either reigns at any given time?

This particular night, as Sabrina swam, she pondered whether the world might be coming to an end. She waited for the Earth to change and waited also, perhaps, for her own salvation.

Suddenly, the impossible happened. A star fell directly in front of her into the cool, mystical waters. Its ravenous, mercurial light split off into myriad prismatic realities. These realities, with their silvery, quick currents created a wave of rippling ebony manes across the umber waters, dropping invisible roots that thirsted for a deep connection to the aquatic realm into which they had fallen.

As these roots spread their tendrils, they unified the heavens with the Earth. Sabrina, a pagan creature, flowered into a state of rapturous wonder. Her soul traveled deeply into the newborn roots as they reached farther into the primal waters. This birthing became all-devouring—a dream breathing her.

The enraptured Sabrina suddenly found herself re-surfacing from the depths of the ebony pool of the night's caves. She wondered if there were one less star now in the heavens. Or if she had embodied the fallen star before its journey back to the night's glittering fields, re-planting its hybrid pulse into the unknowable eternities. She had seen through the star's eye, gazed through that illumination into a luminous twin self. And now, she too was changed, transformed from this mysterious, wild symbiosis with distant worlds, other selves revealed.

Ever to be bedazzled from this wondrous experience, Sabrina felt the more expansive star of herself illumined. She wondered if the heavens' star had actually fallen—or whether it was all a vision of a deeper reflection, a dive into the oceanic wilderness of the unconscious.

2002

GALACTIC HYMNS

O Stars that tumble
into my heart, bathing me
with ancient heavenly light,
you sing beyond the mind.

You heal the root
which has been torn,
seeding my well
with eternal song.

In a flash of light,
you carry me
through space and time,
your galactic hymns
wreathing my soul
with ceaseless radiance.

O Stars strewn across
the nocturnal dome,
I pause in wonder
at the mystery
behind your splendor.

2010

GOSSAMER MEMORIES

Last night we were breathed by the stars, the ancient lords of mystery, the ebony glittering dome. The moon cast silvery plumage upon the surge of tides, bathing us in her unceasing extravagance. The seminal seas roared below, aquatic fields bursting into bloom. Illumined crowns bejeweled the verdant cypress trees. We imbibed the wine of lunar enchantment, the shadows, the flowering seas. As the music of resonant glory currented our veins, our essences blended, and we became more than we had been.

Now, wearing only gossamer memories as our invisible cloaks of blessing, we watch as the fog drifts in, obscuring the heavens, enshrouding the trees with veils of lavender mist. Today's clime holds the cold, damp breath of winter; all is changing, *is* change. And within this cycle lives all the seasons, the unsame of the Same.[25] The gray, torpid heaviness, like undeveloped film, awaits the unknown, the birth of endless forms from the formless.

Bowing to such beauty, we humbly walk on.

2001

YOU AMAZE ME

Wearing a woven spell of kindness,
you amaze me with your presence.

Beaming like the sun,
your golden presence
lifts me into shining realms—
my pulse ignites in your caress.

Possessed by
our erotic embodiment,
we melt into one.

Magically, a white bird,
birthed of the Bible-black night,
sings to us of unseen worlds
that rise now as music in the air,
for our eternal breath.

2010

IN THE GOLDEN LIGHT OF HEALING
for John

Having been on an emotional rollercoaster all day, she rested now in her spacious living room with twilight's coppery light dappling the high redwood beams. Then, after an illuminating visit from her friend and neighbor, Noah, guardian of the animals, birds, and gardens, she felt her sap, her heart's wine revivified.

Noah is a tall, large-winged, eagle-eyed man who embodies an earthy wisdom. And even more important, for the moment, she felt his love and tenderness showered like a river upon her.

True friendship, a blessed mantle, crowned her with jewels, transforming her. She felt as if she were dripping in the gold of genuine kindness. The essence of life returned, flowing through her again.

Before he departed, he held her with the rare and unselfish love of a male angel. He said *she* was the angel because she helped so many people, people she would never know or meet. She just stood there in that river of blessing, which rooted her feet, and she drank again from life's primal wells.

He had restored her to that sacred place because he, too, was an angel on Earth. And their hearts shone together in the golden light of healing.

2007

O CREST OF THE WILD

O lover of my gentlest dreams,
O tides that bejewel my shores,
I discover you in the peacock's wing,
yet also in the brute force of wind.

My heart lies down
upon your feathers, lush,
warmed by the secrets you whisper
to the mossy green of my soul.

And here we are again,
on the crest of the wild,
wandering the early spring meadow.

For now, we live the foam's breath.
That is enough—it holds everything.

2002

OFFERING HERSELF TO THE MYSTERY

for David and D. H. Lawrence

She felt as if reborn, having arrived in the metropolis. Shedding the skins of yesterday's surrealism, she innocently rode the Tao's wave like a valiant, exploring child. Why was she here? What was she doing? All these fear-ignited questions dissolved as she embodied the energy of each moment without expectation, experiencing a new openness. Regaining the chameleon of herself, this child in wonder grew, this savant of the Unknowing. How could she be so blessed? Miracle after miracle revealed itself through her, as the Tao guided her so effortlessly, so exquisitely down dawn's path.

Tonight had been paradisiacal. By offering herself to the Mystery, her deepest desire had been undressed. Her man of the night had appeared so elusively, yet as a fountain rising from the hot earth, from the flames of her unconscious yearnings, effortlessly manifesting the life she had unconsciously desired.

2011

THIS PART OF HER ARM

"This part of my arm," she exclaimed, "is innocent, untouched. It has never been part of the world. It thrives in childhood's bramble and bees, in the fawn, the visiting bird and the light-heartedness of youth. Yes, this part of my arm," she repeated, "is innocent."

Then he kissed her little hand and sprinkled water on her dear, little arm. And she became innocent again.

2007

A STORY WITHOUT A TALE

for Nikos Kazantzakis

She felt an urge within her, an insistent thrust to spill out a tale, although she knew not what shape it would take. She would let the blood of her pen's ink write, re-create her out of the formless into another myth.

In this balmy, liberating afternoon of epiphanies, Sequentia carefully climbed over endless mounds of rocks to walk the long stretch of pristine beach ahead. She whistled to the soaring droves of pelicans flying in their instinctive, synchronized patterns, while the red-beaked seagulls in their immaculate, feathered attire eyed her.

Wearing pink ballet shoes, Sequentia scampered along the sandy shores, running with the tides as the golden sunbeams shone upon her auburn tresses. Never before had she experienced the sea with such wonder. She sensed the treachery of its unbounded power as her own, as the very core of all breathing things. Respectful of the tides, she observed their cyclical drift, knowing the surging currents could trap her if she miscalculated their timing or direction.

On her way back from the beach, Sequentia found a stone cave that protected her from the sunset winds. Reclining against a rock, she began reading *Saviors of God* by Nikos Kazantzakis. How it fed her soul to read this fervent poet's cry. How greedily she devoured the dead master's entrails, his spirit, his soul-embodied words. How his word-flames seared her heart, re-lighting the candles of her dark journey into reverence.

She felt Nikos reach out and reconnect her to the marrow of her ancestors, to all humankind. She could envision the innumerable pilgrims walking in darkness throughout time across the deserts of the dead. Their sublime mission of transfusing the density of matter into spirit, of transmigration, could be traced to our very origins. How it expanded her vision to reach back into the deep, screaming roots of humankind, to peer into the Earth's endless graves, to sense the rivers of their blood, feeding, watering, guiding us across the infinite seas of universal dreams and lament.

The bones and skulls of our ancestors, she pondered, may now be but powder; nevertheless, the ferment of their hearts and spirits burn on through us. We consume the richness of their spirits in the sacred art they leave behind, laughing, weeping their songs and screams as our own. Their season after death pulses through our veins, using our flesh now for their sustenance, giving them immortality through us. Today, we are their endless streams of coffin-bearers, purposeful cemeteries on legs. Through the centuries, they triumphantly discard their bodies, leaving us the promise of reincarnation through another man's seed and another woman's fruit. Their tree of death, when lovingly watered with our own pulsing spirit-streams, blossoms their golden fruit in undying seasons. As their slaves, we feed them our living blood, transfusing their fleshless sacraments, which we now embody, offering them and ourselves this salvation.

Sequentia wrote, "How thrilled I am to have Nikos inhabit me. He can drink my blood and camp in the caverns of my wilderness-brain for as long as he likes, for he has revitalized my spirit's grasses, flooded them with the essence they long for. I am drunk with inspiration, the ambrosia of his wine of origin."

Hours later, Sequentia was lying on her pink cloud of a bed with *Saviors of God* opened across her breast. She reflected on what a sacred gift art can be, coming to us from beyond the illusion of time and space. Like a ceaseless, unbroken pulse of past generations, the essence of these spiritual masters bursts forth through the Earth, through us as the chosen fountains of their expression and continuation. Who now is dead or alive? Aren't we all part of this unbroken pulse, forms changing with the seasons, rising and falling within the continuum through the light and dark of this planet's flashing organism?

We are called upon to reunite beyond the wars and strife, to ascend the limitations of our ephemeral flesh. The darkness is filled with the cries and joys of countless poets and warriors whose blazing flames light our candles with the treasures they leave behind. And we, without remorse, so feed them now with the ignited passion and visceral nature of our flesh-filled present intentions.

Sequentia knew this tale-less story was fathered by Nikos. What might have remained an unborn seed had sprouted into a wildflower, inspired and fertilized by the immortality of his protean soul.

2002

MUSIC FROM ANOTHER TIME

Wearing an ancestor's face,
the moon casts a silvery path
welcoming her fate.

And the priestess
lies down with her lover,
exchanging complexions.

On a velvet couch,
the song of love holds hands
with a dead violin
while music from another time
enters through a closed window
then twirls around her second shoe,
which hides in shame
from her last rendezvous.

Yet, who can find her
now that she joined the monastery?
And who can climb a mountain
as steep as hers?

Only a black crow befriends her.
Is she lost to the music
of another time?

Or is life more assertive
than the drudgery of logic?

And are the wings
of unspoken destiny
waiting to fly her higher,
to a wider fate?

2009

The Yak of My Soul

MY INTIMATE COMPANION

Riding the black mule of condescension, I descend into the stony ravines of contemplation. Is this *really* living? This life apart from what others live, as they busily travel here and there, as they laugh and do a myriad of external things? In these ravines and at the summits it is all about experimentation and discovery, a way of communing with my soul and the universe at large, an adventure of letting life be, of letting destiny vibrate. These unutterable sensings emanate from an ancient peasant within, some timeless entity who knows without knowing, who is simple, who penetrates the blue of sky, the cobalt heart of the sea.

This peasant climbs to the peaks and chuckles at the obscenities of being human, mocking our ironies and absurdities with a lucid indifference. His enduring courage gives him the depth of understanding necessary to die repeatedly before the complete death. Yes, this timeless peasant becomes my intimate companion, unannounced, guiding my windy soul along the rocky cliffs. He is an invisible companion because he has been so blown about by the winds of time that he avoids more exposure.

Yes, this omniscient one, this invisible third eye, will guide the unmarked path to death, to the numerous deaths along an ever-widening road that someday will open to the vast mouth of oblivion. Yes, he will be my companion to the end with the eagle's eye and the arms of night to comfort, to guide the black mule's ascent.

2007

HER SHADOW MANIFESTS

Amanda, a young-at-heart though aging courtesan, had been the lover of many a stately man. Over the years she had managed to amass a small fortune, which she had systematically stashed away. She had probably inherited the instinct to preserve and accumulate from her father, an expert at running a tight ship, as he would say. Then again, she could also be most generous with her money and feelings, perhaps due to the genetic inheritance from her artistic and philanthropic mother. But somehow, in her desire to preserve her enormous wealth, she had manifested a most dangerous situation.

The problem seemed to begin when a certain Ms. Miriam Bear encouraged Amanda to place a large amount of cash in a bank vault for a possible emergency. After all, since 9/11, and with the world's ever-increasing bloodshed and terrorism, no one felt safe. So with Ms. Bear's assistance, Amanda made arrangements to meet with the bank officials after closing hours.

On the appointed day, Amanda quickly dressed in embroidered blue jeans and a bright red T-shirt, arriving exactly on time. Miriam was already there, waiting at the elevator. They were greeted by two bank officers with a guard who, pushing a cart with an enormous satchel, escorted them into the underground vaults. Although congenial, the three male employees were also aloof and militant.

With the new vault key in hand, Amanda turned her back to them as she sought to unlock the heavy safe. But just as she put the key in the lock, she felt a rough poke from the back. Alarmed, she twirled around, coming face to face with a masked man shoving a revolver into her ribs. Of course she was terrified and instantly looked to the bank officers for help, but they too were stricken with fear. The robber, who was short and stocky and dressed completely in white, held guns in both hands: one which he continued to jab into her ribs and another which he directed at the bank employees.

Pushing her out of the subterranean vault with the butt of his gun, he handcuffed and seat-belted her into his car parked nearby. Curiously, when he turned on his CD player, an evangelist was preaching, but Amanda, overwhelmed with anguish, missed the irony of this. He drove quickly and abruptly, repeatedly assuring her that he would not harm her. Finally, they reached a remote wilderness area, high in the mountains, surrounded by the summer's drying grasses. After slamming on the brakes, he yanked her out and roughly tied her to the handle of the closed car door. Then he went to the trunk and unloaded a large, steel coffin, which resembled the huge bank safe. Furiously, he began digging in the dry dirt for what felt like eons to Amanda, who was, of course, still in a state of terror.

The sun was scorching, the air raspingly dry. Amanda prayed he would fall from exhaustion from digging such a fathomless hole in the torpid heat. But this bovine man dressed in white was a tough, determined little beast. Finally, a few hours after twilight, when darkness had swallowed them, he looked her directly in the eyes and commanded that she jump into the gruesome steel box now laid in the deep, dark earth.

She shuddered and screamed, "You said you wouldn't hurt me." He hissed like a rattlesnake and retorted mockingly: "No, it won't be me who hurts you." At that, he shoved her and she tripped on the rocky terrain, falling on top of the pile of cash she had preserved for an emergency. It surrounded her like so many dry leaves. She continued to shriek as this lunatic buried her body, her money, her life.

He bellowed from above her grave, "I don't want one cent of your fortune. I am only your shadow, summoned by your soul, to make your impossible dream possible. Yes, you *can* take it with you, but it will cost you your life."

She wept and closed her eyes. "Thank you," she gasped with her last breath. And her nightmare abruptly ended.

2007

ANASTASIA
for Nikos Kazantzakis

On Independence Day, the moon rose pink from the fever of the day. Anastasia scrutinized the movie reel of her lengthy, charmed life. Images of ancestors, lovers, friends reincarnated through her like invisible ghosts wailing, moaning, drinking blood at the well of her soul.

Suddenly, she began to see herself and other living creatures as curiously diverse, incoherent organisms in transition, chameleons ever shedding old skins. Like lightening, this revelation struck every molecule of her being.

Anastasia had been born a contrarian; it was inherent in the acorn of her nature. Sometimes the seesaw of her contrary selves rode her up and down between archetypal forces, which could cancel each other out, resulting in a limbo of ambivalence. The polarities of her existence called to mind her deceased parents, who were opposite in nature. She had accustomed herself to these irreconcilable traits, even accepted them, recognizing the creativity ignited by their churn.

To find, not to seek, was her way, seeded by her reverence for the Tao and its profound mystery. Anything that disrupted the sacred and timeless, puncturing the resonance, was blasphemous to the numinous realms. Anastasia was devoted to discovering through life's media the symbolic meanings of mystical metaphors, the irony and satire of the synchronicities of the Tao. She knew she was on the right path when the miracles magically manifested like tumbleweeds blown by eternal winds. When they *found* her, they were often embodied in her art, where they rose to the surface as poetic images offering an interactive mirror of her discarded skins. But first she had to create a silent, sacred space in which these revelations or epiphanies could occur, a realm that gave breath to her soul's vulnerability, the invisible instrument of invention.

Later, when these impressions had fermented into consciousness, she could weigh, prune, enrich, distort, shape, or embellish them as she saw fit. But the exulted soul, impassioned by the wild herds of the senses, preceded any analysis that may have followed. Ah, what seminal joy to transpose experience through art, metabolizing a lyrical language which could feed and liberate the spirit. In this mystical way, the bloodstream of the Tao transmuted the clay of her flesh into spirit.

She understood that the polarities of aversion and attraction were innate, fueled by the Indestructible Entity. The interior climates of her enigmatic self spoke of the constancy of the inconstant, the paradoxes she continually felt as a misfit amongst the sterile conformists. Her inner mosaic, her rich tapestry of inherited and acquired traits was gradually manifesting, revealing her inner fabric to her many selves, others, and the world.

Anastasia gazed with both horror and compassion at the soulless desert of contemporary times, the rapid deterioration and suffering. As if in tragic mockery, a new, yet dying world dangled before her, lost in transition. Brainwashed by propaganda, driven by fear and greed, the depersonalized human appeared programmed to live a life of mechanized enslavement.

She had known the forces of the patriarchal systems intimately. Having been exposed to her father's wealth and tyranny, it was even more essential years ago that she break free, sculpt her own character, discover her essence apart from his oppression and the world's ruthless systems.

Even though she had moved to a mountaintop far away, she saw there was no escape from the world's ironic and persistent dynamics. Born of the flames of existence, the cosmic forces consistently took the form of challenges bargaining for her soul. These energies required her vigilant scrutiny as they masqueraded before and through her, wearing innumerable masks. The tides of her soul longed to reconnect, to drink from the seas of the unconditioned again. And apparently the world needed to as well.

Anastasia recognized that the archetypal themes that had chiseled their way into her consciousness were the same challenges facing the world at large. She understood that the forces use humanity as tools for evolution, for so-called progress, that destruction is also an essential ingredient of metamorphosis, that this refining through abrasion[26] is the grist of the Earth's mill.

She could see through her own joys and struggles and those of humankind to the underlying polarities, the seething cauldron in its ever-changing scenarios. She observed how the literal interpretation of external events and behaviors could trap her in a myopic cul-de-sac of fear and ignorance, whereas viewing life from an expanding cosmogonic perspective could help her to transcend duality by liberating her spirit beyond Earth's gravity.

Anastasia recognized that art, music, dance, and meditation could also cultivate this expanded perspective by integrating the myriad facets of our lives into higher purposes, orchestrating the instincts into harmonious resonance. While Nature doesn't create everyone to be an artist or monk, all can be motivated by what Nikos terms *the noble passion,* the thrust to spiritualize matter.[27] In this way, rather than bringing out savage behavior, instincts can be integrated with higher consciousness.

Anastasia found little evidence of this change in the world, which appeared to grow ever more complex and decadent. Isn't the universe continuously revolving in cycles of death and rebirth? Don't the light and dark forces relentlessly orchestrate the Circus, while the Eternal Kiln of Death devours us indifferently? And can violence ever cease when it is such an integral part of birth? Isn't this futile, yet miraculous way the inherent pulse of the Earth's soul?

How could the Earth's blood ever be changed except first within the individual? If enough individuals sought their kingdom within, and united, perhaps the world could change. Such are the thoughts of cloud-dreamers and anarchists, she speculated.

Anastasia proclaimed: Let us acknowledge the infinite flame behind the soul's relentless incarnations and the body's ultimate ashes. May we live like the silkworm that consumes mulberry leaves, produces silk, and then devours its inner chambers before finally ascending. May we offer the butterfly that we toil to become to this infinite flame, valiantly feeding ourselves into the ever-expanding incinerator without the bias of hope or the subterfuge of escape.

On this Independence Day, Anastasia could now rest, after realizing independence means liberation from attachment and misdirected desire, transposing matter into spirit as one's noble passion.

2003

FREE OF DESIRE

Ah, tonight is a night free of desire
for anything but what is.
Yes, tonight even
secret longings sleep.

Tonight I embrace the gentle breeze
as my own breath,
and the sparkling lights
of ancient constellations
guide my heart.

A waning moon shimmers
in the black lagoon
as a sovereign sister,
and jets tear through
saintly kingdoms of night.

Yes, tonight is a night free of desire
for anything but what is.

The powerful land I inhabit
and the roaring sea below
are one with my throbbing pulse—
an extension of me
in the liberated moment.

2008

CLEOPATRA'S REBIRTH

Cleopatra removed her crown, breathed a deep sigh, and reclined on the tender grasses of her small garden. She felt continually challenged to try to satisfy the public's expectations. What did her heart really feel? She had employed the two sturdy steeds of Indifference and Detachment to assist her through these difficult times: the war and struggle inherent in the seething cauldron of existence. Yet recently these adaptations felt so dehumanizing that she missed her more exalted states.

As she reminisced, Augustus, her beloved cat, sauntered by and wrapped his black, serpentine tail around her left ankle. What fertile passion she felt for this aloof, black-and-white creature. His gold eyes, usually furtive, gazed steadily at her. She was in a trance-like state as her vision swept the moody desert skies, where the half-smile of a crescent moon seemed to reflect her thoughts, even mutely to answer them. She wondered if the moon was lonely in its solitary orbit. Did it ever feel as she did, locked into a life-sentence of solitary confinement?

Just then, the orchestration of countless crickets began to fill the pulsing Egyptian night. The beat began to swell. Her golden-eyed cat meowed, and Cleopatra fell further into a dream-like swoon. A fragrance of wild lilac and jasmine intoxicated her senses. She reflected on her life and on her father, who was a continual source of strife as his opposite nature rubbed against her grain unmercifully. Her father was the Pharaoh, the willful and brilliant leader of the Egyptian people. Cleopatra was unmarried and his only daughter. And like an exotic pet, he adored her with an oddly indifferent passion, yet greatly depended upon her. She wondered if she could ever escape this destiny that hung like an invisible yoke around her neck.

Numerous times she had questioned the meaning of destiny. Wasn't it a kind of Braille, circumscribed by the blind forces, which although invisible, could nonetheless be scrutinized from a variety of angles? By studying one's genetics and environment, one could begin to see certain patterns emerge. How could she be sure that her being would flower even if she did manage somehow to disentangle from the power struggle with her father?

Cleopatra was aware not only of her father's extremely competitive nature and tyrannical drive to govern the masses—but also of his attempts to rule her soul. All her life they had been in a silent war. She knew enough from her studies and contemplation to recognize that she and her father represented the polarities, the pendulum of opposites in their eternal swing. But if she deserted him (and he was nearly ninety years old), would she just find herself facing the same challenges in other forms?

Over the years, she had learned to detach from phenomena and observe. She had also repeatedly taken her power back by not allowing herself to express the fury that at times overwhelmed her. She noticed how acting out her anger only seemed to empower him and leave her drained. At those times, she limped about, hollow, emotionally distraught—her murdered soul dragged around her feet like a ball and chain.

As Cleopatra climbed down the labyrinthine ladder of her psyche's excavations she looked to the moon for answers, but it was now eclipsed by an ominous gray mist. Cleopatra finally understood that she didn't have to show up for the power struggle. She could disengage, but didn't that stance become its own spiritual pawn? What happens to intimacy and passion if one becomes too practiced in detachment? Through her understanding of human nature and the world, Cleopatra also knew that she too possessed inscrutable tyrants that chewed on the flowers of her inner kingdom. How much of her struggle with her father was caused by him—how much by herself? Perhaps she too was a warrior. The hierarchies that tyrannized her brain were to be seen through and dismantled, freeing her from the determination of stale habit. She glanced up again at the ancient moon that now seemed to smile, confirming her reflections.

Wisps of feathery mist drifted away from the moon, as if with a secret purpose. Cleopatra had observed the games of the mind and the caprice of nature as the unyielding host. She observed that in a power struggle, one is always more dominant than another at any given time. Or do the two participants eventually end up the same, she wondered, like life and death? Cleopatra didn't want to assume one role or the other. She preferred a duet—a dance of complementary yield.

Suddenly she was overwhelmed with grief at the recent loss of one of her favorite cats. She cried out to him to fill the shadow of his vanished presence in the ebony night. "Oh, black-furred Basil, handsome moon-cat of the wilderness desert, my love keeps you nearby, impassions your light eternal. Come here, dearest creature of my soul," she wailed. "Stalk by me in the night with your solitary nature and your white fur to the knee. Walk by me, and let me love you madly and forever in the night's bitter passion and fragrance. Just let me love you madly," she wept again.

She sensed his unseen presence and felt his wild spirit as her own. Just then, as she gazed above her, the glitter of distant stars wreathed the once solitary moon. Entranced, she felt as if she herself were another star in cadence with the galactic splendor.

For as long as she lived, she would attempt to penetrate the Mystery and its struggles in the great river of the opposing forces. She would explore the great wonders of existence and exalt in the simple joys. Cleopatra owed it to the world and to her ancestors and out of necessity to herself. For now, she yielded to her destiny, knowing that at any instant her life could change.

After continually probing her heart for answers, she became more aware of her enigmatic moods and thoughts and realized that truth is altogether transitory. Her way was to live the moment's wonders guided by sublime intuition, beyond knowing, trusting the Mystery. Although she knew her Earth time was evanescent, she felt her essence as being eternal.

The smiling moon had now moved away, filled with revelation, as it appeared to Cleopatra on that breathless desert evening long ago. Reborn by her latest insights, she reveled in newfound freedom, vowing to embody the emerging realm in her heart with the intensity of her dreams.

2006

THE PILLOWS OF ETERNITY

Through the blue silence of twilight,
a gentle rain falls,
moistening the yearning land.
I rest on the pillows of eternity,
gazing out to the seamless horizon.

Worlds reached expand
and dissolve autonomously.

Like an explorer,
I follow the dawn-lit path
leading to ancient realms
of dying stars in rebirth.

In the metallic splendor
of this glittering chaos,
I find my soul
and bask in the infinitudes,
resting on the pillows of eternity
without desire or plan.

And the soft summer rain
continues to fall,
anointing the path with dew
for my tomorrow.

2011

NEBULOUS INSCAPE

O Earth, how torn from you I am. The heavens beyond seem closer than your deep fecundity. In the gasping ethers of the city, in the climes tainted with human discomfort, I drift as a dry leaf in autumn, between the untouched realms of the ephemeral and the abyss of the unconscious— where the ugly gods of paranoia, betrayal, and victimization hide. Having no fear of this peculiar ambiguity, I allow myself to dissolve into the formlessness of a neutral sea.

From this state of suspension, I recall the time when I gazed into the eyes of my dying pet bird and knew of more than mortality. And I became larger for this. The dying into this dear little creature's eyes was among my saddest and bravest experiences. When I died into my father's distant vacancy, it was more living than dying. When I sang into the heart of my dying dog, his eyes taught me more than any book.

And now, in this particularly contemptuous year, I recline, skin-clothed, bathed in mists of moodiness, disinterested in the debates, the competitions of dead yesterdays. After rehashing memories, I toss them to the devouring rats of time, keeping just a scrap of me un-chewed. Now, the rays of past dawns cast static fingers that fade into distant mountains. Even cut flowers seem to wither more quickly in autumn.

My lids rest upon the fresh petals of unknown tomorrows. Ah, what blessedness, this unforeseen rest, this reprieve from scorching suns and galloping heart. I huddle inside a nest of woven, emerald grasses within, inviting selves to shed their outworn skins, to vanish into the reeds, seeding my renewal.

1996

O NIGHT, MY EBONY MASTER

in memory of beloved Edmund Kara

O night, whose darkness I inhabit, let the seeds that thrive in your womb of sea inseminate me, resurrecting me as the bud before spring.

O darkness, that feeds my blindness with vision, come to me this night; embody my dreams.

Come to me, wingéd ebony lord, master of my flesh's glory. Come to me, infuse my desert garden with your fragrance. Embody my ghosts with your tawny arms like dappled boughs dancing in the warm breeze.

I await you, dearest master of my dry heart's love. If I appear asleep, I only pretend, because under my many-petaled lids lives my rose of love. And that hidden half of love wants you now, in all your contained splendor, to bathe me in your oceans of birth, to wing my blanched shoulders before the dawn.

How long shall I wait, O seeds of night, O ebony sky that yearns for dawn? Or will the world of denser matter never free your wings to me, but cage you in an aviary upon a mountain tall?

Will the windstorms tear down these walls that hold you captive, at last freeing you to me—like an eagle soaring high, eyeing his prey? Predator or prey, which will you be to me and I to thee? Or neither shall we be?

The night swims on, leaving me to obscurity. I close my light and then my lids, wearily awaiting sleep. Perhaps you'll sing to me in dream this night, O ebony master of unknown stars to be. Perhaps my soul will be fed your pollen invisibly.

As the paper is filled, my pen runs dry, and my blood feels heavy, yet pale.

O phantom, O lord, O seed, O husk, bring your tawny arms to me while on Earth we still be.

2001

BURSTING WITH SECRETS

Stray reflections vagrantly drift
across the twilight sea.

Drowsy mountains
dip rocky toes
into the singing sea,
growing black in
the cascading darkness.

And the harvest moon
threatens to burst with
all her silvery secrets,
letting them fall to earth
like love letters written
to our beseeching souls.

2011

HELEN, THE SPARTAN QUEEN, RESURRECTED

After completing a painting titled *Helen, the Spartan Queen, Resurrected,* I began to discover her symbolic significance in my own life. For months, the gods at sea had dashed me ruthlessly against the white, rocky cliffs. How long had this odyssey lasted? I hadn't written a story in my journal for three months. Where had I been?

Now, on this first day of my retreat, I wonder what enriching fibers might interweave with my soul, seducing the muse to return.

I sit on an old, wooden bench—facing the timeless sea, watching the whales as they breech on their trek to Mexico. Nearby, black-and-yellow furry bumblebees sip pollen from a flower whose colors match theirs. Vines of fading blue wisteria cascade over the bedroom deck while a few buzzing bees sip the last of their sultry wine. And the lazy mountain peaks slumber in veils of honey-green twilight. An ultimate day is ending, under a sliver of moon now emerging.

Is it possible to capture this day, its varied essence? How can I preserve this silence and beauty? I could tell everyone that this is a monastery, that monks live here, that we should speak as little as possible. I'd actually be doing all of us a favor by imposing this restraint. There's such an abundance of chatter and noise in our world today. It's as if our anxiety, wearing the mask of purpose, acts like a monster and devours our most precious possession—silence.

The comedy of our cosmic pageant makes me laugh at the irony and absurdity of our meaningless pantomimes. Forces fuel us while we, as pathetic puppets attached to our myths and masks, let our manifestations define us. What a tragic joke.

The bees continue to sip from their matching flowers as if to mock my complex musings. We are all honeybees with a calling. And like bees, we have our specialized purposes, yet our energies extend far beyond our focus, continually influencing everyone and everything around us and accomplishing other feats of which we are often unaware. For instance, the artist not only creates works of art but in so doing also adds invisible yet vital ingredients to the energy fields at large.

A gauzy moon casts suffused light on the fathomless shadows, easing the torments of noon. A diaphanous shroud of mist falls like a hush over the ebony seas. Yet I am still breathing in the day's warmth that lingers now in the night's infusions.

I hadn't heard the breath of the ocean for ages. How far away I had roamed. Now, a distant, muffled roar fills the beach coves below. I imagine I am a priestess, high upon a summit of ever-revealing realms.

My home offers me shelter inside its mute, redwood walls. Its once-lost vitality has been restored.

My paintings, the pink, cozy bed, the candles, the sacred objects, have all become interwoven chords of harmony and integration. A resonance so longed-for is mine again, a sublime gift of these golden hours of solitude.

Listening to the lyrical tides caress the shores, I discover freshly bathed shells strewn about, and I revel in hitherto unheard melodies.

2007

I FOUND MY SOUL

for Laura Archera Huxley

In the grace of
a dying garden,
I found my soul.

In the crisp, golden leaves,
in the broken tile,
under the arches of a dead history,
my soul appeared, naked amid
the crumbling tower of yesterday.

In the shady nooks,
secrets lie with blue lips
waiting to be revived
by a red generation.

I swim in the old pool
with new water and
the light of the future
beams through boughs
of ancient oak.

Old and new fuse
in my bloodstreams—
in the primal waters.

2007
inspired by a swim at the Hollywood Hills home of Laura Huxley

NOTES

1. PAGE 24—*meme,* unit of information passed from one person or group to another
2. PAGE 46—as demonstrated in the film, *What the Bleep Do We Know!?*
3. PAGE 46—"Tower of Song" by Leonard Cohen
4. PAGE 47—*survival instincts* from the theory of survival emotions in *Exo-Psychology* by Timothy Leary (1920–1996), friend, philosopher, psychologist, professor, author
5. PAGE 47—*will to power* from *Thus Spake Zarathustra* by Friedrich Nietzsche (1844–1900)
6. PAGE 62—inspiration for this story from Albert Camus, *Lyrical and Critical Essays,* Philip Thody (ed.), Ellen Conroy Kennedy (tr.)
7. PAGE 64—Found in Australia and New Guinea, the bowerbird is known for its unusual behavior of creating an elaborate bower-like nest, often decorated with colorful objects and sometimes painted with plant juice to attract a mate.
8. PAGE 70—*wild goats of the senses* from *Report to Greco,* the autobiography of Nikos Kazantzakis
9. PAGE 79—*unsame of the Same* from the late Michelle Ryan, friend, poet
10. PAGE 80—*abrasion for refinement* from Benjamin De Casseres (1873–1945), poet, novelist, playwright, journalist, philosopher
11. PAGE 86—*refinement through abrasion*—See Note 10.
12. PAGE 87—*barometers of the Earth's consciousness* attributed to Maurice Maeterlinck (1862–1949), Nobel prize-winning poet, naturalist, a favorite of Hermann Hesse
13. PAGE 87—*unsame of the Same*—See Note 9.
14. PAGE 96—*forces of history dressed up* from Benjamin De Casseres (1873–1945), poet, philosopher, novelist, playwright, journalist
15. PAGE 96—*archaic revival* from Terence McKenna (1946–2000), friend, biologist, scholar, author, teacher
16. PAGE 116—for Laura Archera Huxley (1913–2007), beloved friend, author of *You Are Not the Target* and *This Timeless Moment: A Personal View of Aldous Huxley*
17. PAGE 141—*wild goats of the senses*—See Note 8.
18. PAGE 141—*blood consciousness* attributed to D. H. Lawrence
19. PAGE 148—in *Lyrical and Critical Essays* by Albert Camus, Philip Thody (ed.), Ellen Conroy Kennedy (tr.)
20. PAGE 174—*"black mania"* referenced by Nikos Kazantzakis in his novel *The Rock Garden*
21. PAGE 174—*blood consciousness*—See Note 18.
22. PAGE 182—*wild goats of the senses*—See Note 8.
23. PAGE 182—*Pankosmion,* Greek, where everything is; a unification of heaven and earth
24. PAGE 183—quotes of Kazantazakis and Prevalakis from *Nikos Kazantzakis and His Odyssey: A Study of the Poet and the Poem* by Pandelis Prevelakis (1909–1986), poet, playwright, professor, long-term friend and disciple of Kazantzakis
25. PAGE 193—*unsame of the Same*—See Note 9.
26. PAGE 207—*refining through abrasion*—See Note 10.
27. PAGE 207—*noble passion* and *spiritualize matter* and related references from *Toda Raba* by Nikos Kazantzakis

PAINTINGS

ABOUT THE AUTHOR

Born in Catford, England, Carolyn grew up in southern California, where she studied art and psychology at UCLA. In 1980 she moved to her cliff-side home high above the Pacific Ocean in Big Sur, where she studies, writes, and paints amidst the surrounding wilderness.

A passion for creative expression and a lifelong fascination with spiritual transformation have propelled Carolyn to become an award-winning poet, writer, and artist. Her eleven books have been used as inspirational texts in universities and healing centers, and are featured along with the writings of seven other acclaimed woman writers in a continuing course, "The Other Half of the Sky: Eight Woman Writers," at Swansea University in Wales. Carolyn's books have been nominated for The Pushcart Prize. Her first book, *Climates of the Mind,* was translated into Braille by the Library of Congress. Her writings have been translated into Korean, Romanian, Arabic, and Bulgarian. Bilingual English-Korean editions of *Soul Seeds: Revelations and Drawings* and *Vagabond Dawns* will be published in the fall of 2012.

Over the past three decades, Carolyn has created an extensive and diverse body of paintings and drawings, ranging in style from romantic figurative to abstract. The Frederick R. Weisman Museum of Art at Pepperdine University exhibited a retrospective of Carolyn's paintings and drawings in 2008 and published a catalog, *Carolyn Mary Kleefeld: Visions from Big Sur,* with commentary by Michael Zakian, PhD, curator and director. Carolyn's art is featured internationally in galleries, museums, private collections, and multimedia presentations.

PO Box 370
Big Sur, California 93920
800-403-3635
831-667-2226

info@carolynmarykleefeld.com
www.carolynmarykleefeld.com

Friend Carolyn Mary Kleefeld on Facebook

BY AND ABOUT CAROLYN MARY KLEEFELD

Poet to Poet #4: Poems—East Coast/West Coast (poems)
With Stanley H. Barkan
The Seventh Quarry/Cross-Cultural Communications, Swansea, Wales and Merrick, NY 2010

Vagabond Dawns (poems, with CD)
Foreword by David Wayne Dunn, Prologue by Professor-Doctor Bernfried Nugel
Cross-Cultural Communications, Merrick, NY 2009

Soul Seeds: Revelations and Drawings (philosophical aphorisms and art)
Foreword by Laura Archera Huxley
Cross-Cultural Communications, Merrick, NY 2008

Carolyn Mary Kleefeld: Visions from Big Sur (catalog from exhibit, Frederick R. Weisman Museum of Art)
Art with commentary by Michael Zakian, PhD
Pepperdine University, Malibu, CA 2008

Kissing Darkness: Love Poems and Art (poems and art)
Co-authored with David Wayne Dunn
RiverWood Books, Ashland, OR 2003

The Alchemy of Possibility: Reinventing Your Personal Mythology
(prose, poetry, and art, with quotes from the Tarot and *I Ching*; can serve as an oracle)
Foreword by Laura Archera Huxley
Merrill-West Publishing, Carmel, CA 1998

Mavericks of the Mind: Conversations for the New Millennium
(interviews with Allen Ginsberg, Terence McKenna, Timothy Leary, Laura Archera Huxley, Carolyn Mary Kleefeld, *et al.*)
By David Jay Brown and Rebecca Novick
The Crossing Press, Freedom, CA 1993; 2nd edition by Maps, Santa Cruz, CA 2010

Songs of Ecstasy, Limited Edition (poems)
Atoms Mirror Atoms, Carmel, CA 1990

Songs of Ecstasy
(art booklet with poems commemorating Carolyn's solo exhibition and poetry reading at Gallerie Illuminati, Santa Monica, CA)
Atoms Mirror Atoms, Carmel, CA 1990

Lovers in Evolution (poems and photographs from Mt. Palomar Observatory)
The Horse and Bird Press, Los Angeles, CA 1983

Satan Sleeps with the Holy: Word Paintings (poems)
The Horse and Bird Press, Los Angeles, CA 1982

Climates of the Mind (poems and philosophical aphorisms)
The Horse and Bird Press, Los Angeles, CA 1979 (4th printing)